Spanish Marmalade

Zindabad's Travels in Spain

Shaukat Khan

*Cover Design, Text and Illustrations copyright
©2011 Shaukat Khan*

*First Edition Published in Great Britain in July 2011
By Khan Art Studio*

ISBN 978-0-9559474-3-8

The right of Shaukat Khan to be identified as Author and Artist of this work has been asserted by him in accordance with the Copyright, Designs and Patents Act 1988

All illustrations, paintings, photographs and sketches by Shaukat Khan

*All rights reserved.
No part of this publication may be reproduced, stored in a retrieval system, or transmitted, in any form or by any means without the prior written permission of the Author.*

*Available from www.khanart.co.uk
Available from all major retailers and available to order through all UK bookshops.*

*Or contact:
Khan Art Studio,
P.O. Box 1008
Canterbury, CT1 9FF
Kent, UK.*

*Email: info@khanart.co.uk
www.khanart.co.uk*

Khan Art Studio's policy is to use papers that are natural, renewable and recyclable products that are made from wood grown in a sustainable forest wherever possible.

Spread the Word!
What the public is saying about *Spanish Marmalade*...

'Really crisp writing – Spanish Marmalade *is that enjoyable sort of travelogue that has more in common with Basho's eccentric sort of haikus than the oft-navel-gazing contemporary reads that occasionally crop up on the Bestseller lists.'*
Aaron Simon, Book Editor for www.Bullet-Reviews.com

'Shaukat's Tales, written in his unique and idiosyncratic style, continue to delight and amuse me. I thoroughly recommend this book, which makes a wonderful travel companion.'
Trish Flynn, Art Teacher, Whitstable, UK

'This book provides my daily dose of laughs – I have read it three times already!'
Dr. Anwar Ajaz, Prominent Artist and Writer, Lahore, Pakistan

'I always read this book on the train, I enjoy it so much it comes with me everywhere.'
Alan Gregory, Business Development Advisor, Littlebourne, UK

'You want to read chapter after chapter of the exciting stories, his humour is addictive and he writes with genuine charm.'
Sally Bowler, Nerja, Spain

*'*Spanish Marmalade *is impossible to put down – I keep it by my bed to unwind after a grinding day.'*
Dr. Laurence Green, Dentist, Canterbury, UK

Contents

And So It Begins

Foreword i
A Million Thanks iii
Disclaimer v

Zindabad's Travels in Spain

In Search of a Dream Villa 2
Home(hunting) Alone 5
Found My Jerusalem 11
Exchange of Contract 13
The Yellow Villa 19
My House Caretaker 25
My Art In Spain 27
The Bruce Forsythe Tea Saga 32
The Village Almayate 34
The Dodgy Estate Agent 36
Breakfast With Figs 38
The Honest Estate Agent 40
Human Fog in the Supermarket 44
Daily Chores 46
Tonbridge Station 49
Gluing up the Passport 51
Karen and Miriam's Success 53
The Tony and Sheila Fiasco 55
There's One Born Every Minute 59
Green and Stripy Store 63
Trip to the Rock 66
Hooked 75
Romeria 77
Creepy-Crawly 79
Water Crisis 83

My Depression	86
Kind Boat Lady	88
Dehydration	92
Kitty Love	95
My Garden	98
It's Our Pleasure	101
Joys and Noise	109
Exhibition Highs and Lows	111
The Old Lady Philanthropist	116
Rainbow Anna	119
My Kitchen	122
Drug Drop	124
Jealous Spanish Lover	127
Wind-Up	130
Saint Valentine's Day	132
Wander to Rhonda	138
The Joy of Roaming in Andalucía	140
Flock of Sheep	155
It Drives You Mad	157
Magic Dance	168
Antonio the Wise	170
Nearly Had My Chips	172
Adios	182

Foreword

So how did I, Shaukat Khan, a Punjabi speaking Pakistani from England, come to be having the adventure of seeking a dream home in a sunny paradise?

I was born in Jullunder, Punjab, in 1939 and came to the UK when I was 20, where I set up a home fragrance business.

In 2000, when I was 61, I went to hospital for a blood test, but I collapsed and had a triple heart bypass instead. This is the story of my life following that surgery, after my multi-million pound business collapsed, and after I spent eleven years more in and out of hospital. Eleven angioplasties later and crippled by constant, excruciating chest pains because of nerve damage caused during my heart operations, I found I had a bug – the painting bug.

My father had suppressed it, preferring I study medicine rather than art. Then came the years of raising seven children when life also revolved around a business. But it was there all the time, waiting to surface and, as it turned out in my hour of need, able to suppress the physical pain better than any drugs the doctors gave me.

What did hurt were the English winters. So, with the support of my loving partner, Janet, I decided to seek a sunny second home, somewhere warm where I could paint.

I didn't want much. Somewhere near the beach because I love the sea. Somewhere not too far from the airport in case bad health dictated a quick departure and near the hospital for the same reason. I didn't want to be near holidaymakers (for the sake of peace and quiet) but I needed to be near other houses, just in case I pegged it. I would prefer to be discovered by people rather than flies. And of course, I wanted somewhere cheap and ready for me to move into.

So I set out – with my wish list, my weak heart and my strong determination.

These are the stories of my experiences, my highs and lows, my struggles and my successes and how I found my dream home in an unsuspecting place. A yellow villa in the village of Almayate, in an area called La Axarquia, in the province around Malaga, called Andalucía: the sunny paradise of Spain.

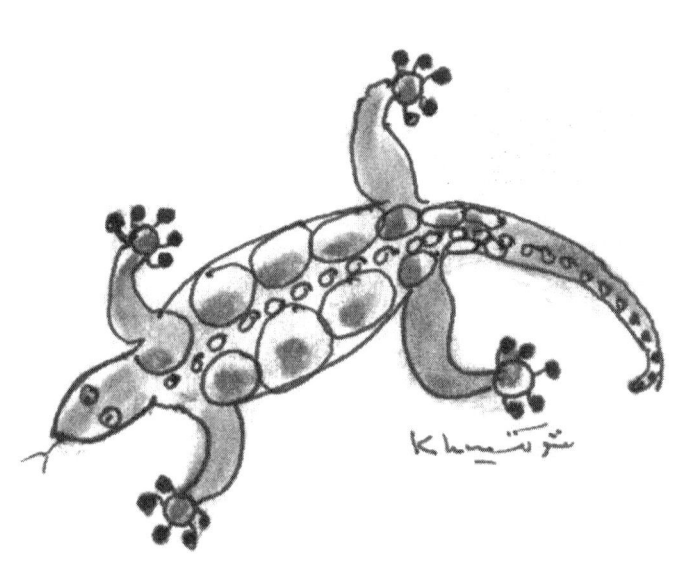

A Million Thanks

Many millions of thanks to Janet Maudsley – the love of my life for 25 years, for her encouragement to go to Spain and find my dream villa was the catalyst to my happiness. For her total devotion, love and care for me in times of crisis, angina attacks and umpteen trips from our home in Canterbury to London Bridge Hospital for several operations, I cannot thank her enough. She is my pillar of strength and without her loyalty, commitment and love; I would not be here to tell these tales.

Thanks to Marnie Summerfield Smith, a talented lady journalist friend. I call her Sparkle because she has a twinkling spirit and shines full of shimmer. She enjoyed my stories and encouraged me to carry on writing despite my dyslexia, which was immensely valuable. She never lost faith in me.

I am so appreciative of Jenny Harrop, who, despite her serious illness, soldiered on to type my manuscript from my badly spoken tapes. She told me she found them so hilarious that she would often have to stop typing due to excessive laughter and take time to dry her tears of joy. She assures me she was laughing with me, not at me.

In Spain, I would like to thank radio stations REM FM and Spectrum FM, especially Spectrum's producer Marco Dalli for his hilarious programme Wind-up. It lifted my spirits when I needed it most. I was also grateful to REM for their invitation to participate in their programme about house hunting in Spain.

Ex-pat magazine *Insight* was also a great source of

information for me personally and while writing this book. I am grateful to editor Malcolm Lewis for his help.

The Junta Andalucia tourist information office in Malaga has provided valuable information on the Axarquia region, its tours and festivals – thank you.

And I would like to thank my local cafe-restaurant, Lo Pepemolina, a place of delicious Spanish food, the brothers Rasheed and Rafique for the unlimited cardamom green tea at the Taj Mahal Indian restaurant at Torre del Mar and all at the beachside makeshift café at Almayate for the grilled fresh sardines. You all made me feel at home.

Also, my Spanish neighbour, Anna Senior – God bless her and may she live one hundred years. She saved my life by fetching her niece, a student nurse, who took me to hospital when I was having an angina attack. It is thanks to the quick thinking of Anna Senior that I can tell this story. Anna Senior's good, neighbourly kindness and generosity extended to looking after and cleaning my house when I was in the UK, as well as doing my laundry and taking care of my precious garden.

I am grateful to Graham Mallaghan for his contribution in checking and improving the manuscript. Finally, thanks to Stephen Yeldham for copy editing the entire book - he is happy to admit that any errors within are now his. Big thanks to all for making this travelogue of mine interesting to readers.

Remember, know what you are seeking, take your time, do not make hasty decisions and always listen to your instincts. Check and double-check the local laws on housing development, which are available from town halls. Always hire a reputable builder or local lawyer, even if you have to pay a little more. The best practice will be to rent a house or villa for a short period and experience and explore the area. If you are happy at the end of a short time, then proceed to look for the property of your dreams.

I dedicate this book to my eldest son, Tippu Badshah Khan, age 44, who died two days before he was to go to Spain with me for the first time, where he would have enjoyed comfort and rest from his illness and had all my fatherly love.

We had such a wonderful trip to Europe when he was six years old. I miss him so much that I have written a novel about our time together. *Farewell My Love* will be published soon.

Enjoy Spanish Marmalade,

Shaukat Zindabad.

Disclaimer and Environmental Statement

These tales are based on true stories but the names and situations are fictitious to safeguard individual privacy. The author has used his imagination to make it interesting for the reader. If there are any coincidences or similarities, then the author apologises in advance.

The publisher and author's policy is to use paper that is natural, renewable and recyclable, made from wood grown in sustainable forests. The logging and manufacturing processes are expected to conform to the environmental regulations of the country of origin.

-1-
In Search of a Dream Villa

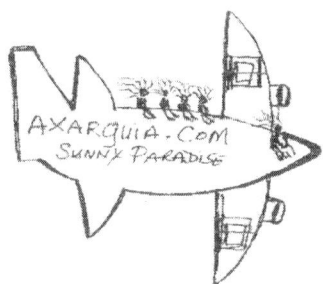

Jan, my partner, had started to nag me about the impact of my wonderful painting paraphernalia.

'Paint on the curtains, charcoal in the carpet, blah, blah, blah.'

I couldn't see where I would do my master painting. I couldn't paint in the kitchen, dining room or drawing room, and we had no spare room.

I had retired early due to illness. I'd had heart operations, stomach ulcers, spinal stenosis but I was just about well enough to paint. I was desperate to indulge this passion that had lain dormant in me for so many decades – but where?

Fed up with worrying about what to do with my life and the frustration of hospitals, doctors, consultants and constant painkillers, I looked for a space outside the house. An old shed would have done, but I had no luck.

Fed up and bored, I took a short break to Torremolinos. Instantly I felt alive. I fell in love with the sandy beaches, palm trees, sunshine, tapas, paella and flamenco dancing. I knew my health and my art would flourish in a place like this.

I came home and told Jan about my plans, then I contacted every Spanish property company I could find. Soon the brochures began arriving. Inspired, I attended the Spanish villa exhibition at Olympia and began making a list.

Needed: 'Three-bedroom villa. Must have garden, swimming pool, car parking and be near the beach, not far from the airport and cheap.'

Was it a hopeless dream?

I made a new list, writing down all the properties I had seen that fitted my requirements and began contacting the estate agents.

'That property has gone but we can offer you something similar.'

How many times did I hear that? Followed by: 'We recommend you book a visit to Spain with us. And bring your chequebook.'

It sounded like a trap to me, but I couldn't resist the temptation – two nights in a three-star hotel with breakfast and flights for £120 per person. I persuaded Jan to come with me.

We arrived at Alicante airport with a lot of enthusiasm (and our chequebook) and stood like two lemons waiting for the estate agent to greet us. We called her after an hour and she suggested we get a taxi to our hotel, as she was unable to meet us for 'personal reasons'. A good start, we thought.

The whole population of England seemed to be waiting in the taxi rank and our enthusiasm for the trip vanished long before the queue did. We arrived at the hotel in Torrevieja expecting the worst, but a welcome from the smiling concierge, a good night's sleep, and a swim in the hotel pool lifted our spirits.

The agent was due to arrive after breakfast. At lunchtime she came, took one look at my list of properties and told me they had all been sold. Three months of hard work and dreaming down the drain.

'But!' she told us (surprise, surprise) 'I have better properties to show you.'

We saw one, and then another one and so on and so on. Some houses she could not find, for others she had no key. They were all too far from the airport and the beach and had no garden or garage. And of course, they were all twice our budget.

Then there were the dream villas that were still in the planning stages.

'You pay a deposit now and in three years it will be yours,' the agent said.

'If I'm still alive,' I thought.

And anyway, all the villas looked the same to me. Row after row of them all the same. Late at night after a few drinks you'd have no chance of finding yours and you'd end up sleeping on the beach.

Our departure from Torrevieja was rather grumpy and glum.

-2-
Home(hunting) Alone

After the fiasco of the Alicante visit, talk of Spain was banned in our house. I had burned my bridges good and proper. So I decided to have one more go – alone.

I found a new estate agent to offer me the property of my dreams. But I had learned my lesson. I was not going to rely on this estate agent to meet me at the airport or even at the hotel after breakfast the following morning. I would take myself to their office and meet them there.

When I arrived, the office was closed.

There was a phone number in the Spanish message stuck on the door, so I called it. A faint and miserable voice answered. It was the estate agent's house. 'Sorry, I'm ill. Come tomorrow?' she said.

I took the opportunity to explore. And soon discovered the area was more like Germany than Spain – dead clean streets, high rise flats, all the signs on the restaurants and shops in German.
'My God!' I thought, 'I will have to learn German as well as Spanish and I haven't learned English properly yet!'

Can you imagine a Punjabi-speaking Pakistani living here, not speaking proper English and not a word of German and Spanish? What a great social life I would have then.

The next morning the estate agent arrived looking sheepish and still grumpy from whatever illness she had. It sounded to me like she had had too much fun at a party.

She made me sit in the corner of the office, where she paid me no attention for nearly an hour, then she bundled me into a 4x4 with a villainous looking man.

'I was head-hunted for this job,' he told me, not smiling.

'I used to work for MI5. I just do this for pocket money. I like you, so stick with me and you'll be all right. There are many dodgy people about.

'Have you brought cash with you? If you like a house, you must put down a deposit straight away. Otherwise, disappointment. A lady came from England last week. She has been looking for a house for 40 years. She found a house she liked, went back to England to get cash – too late. House sold to someone else. So it is very important you have cash with you.'

I nodded. I had already learned that Spain is not like England where you can be gazumped at the last moment. Once you put down a deposit in Spain you are safe.

A few miles and a lecture on Spanish property later, we arrived at a café where I was handed over to another man who spoke no English, German or Punjabi.

He took me to various Spanish village fincas, which had been used to keep goats, sheep and bulls. It was an exhausting and fruitless afternoon. I was delivered back to the estate agent's office where I made an appointment for further punishment the next day.

I went back to the hotel and had dinner with a sense of growing unease. That night I went back to the estate agent's office and put a note through the door, saying 'Gone to England'.

The next day I had a nice lie-in until noon, then I got up, had coffee and started exploring for the property of my own dreams.

I saw various estate agents, got lots of details and found it was the same old story – the same old punishment. But finally, I found an estate agent that spoke English. I explained my requirements and instead of trying to fob me off with any old house he had, he said he didn't have anything right for me, but did I want to leave my number, in case?

I gave him my mobile number and returned to the hotel.

The next morning he rang. He'd found an apartment near the sea, a house near the beach and a village villa just one mile from the beach.

Feeling hopeful I turned up at the office and we went to the first apartment. It was small and didn't fulfil all my requirements but by this point I was so desperate, I was willing to buy. Maybe it could be a stepping-stone to a better property in the future?

I telephoned Jan to tell her the good news and she told me in no uncertain terms that if I were to buy this tiny flat in a German colony that I was not to return to England.

I wanted to stand up to her ultimatum but I am an ill man and need Jan in case I get ill again. I could not go against her wishes. She had given up her job to look after me when I had my heart bypass. She had already spent six months looking after me. It wasn't a matter of pride, just common sense.

So I told the estate agent we would have to go and see the house near the beach. But no luck, the owner was away and there was no chance of seeing inside.

So we were down to the last choice – the villa in the village of Almayate, one mile from the beach.

The estate agent showed me the beach first. It was about five miles long and peaceful, with not a soul to be seen apart from some fishermen and horse riders. There was a little café made from bamboo that served Coca-Cola, ice cream, tea and coffee on plastic tables and chairs.

Then we walked through fields of runner beans, tomatoes, cabbages and lettuces to get to the village and as we approached it, I could see it was surrounded by blue mountains that were covered with groves of avocado pears, wild almonds, palm trees, pomegranates and mangoes. There seemed to be an incredible light and already I could feel my heart going gaga.

Then, amidst the untidy little village, I saw it: A yellow Moorish style villa on two levels with a large balcony looking out to sea. My heart was pounding as the agent unlocked the wrought iron gates and led me through the courtyard garden. Inside, everything was tiled in marble. There was a large drawing room, big kitchen and a laundry room with toilet. A beautifully carved wooden banister curved round the staircase, leading from the dining room to a large upstairs landing, two big bedrooms, the bathroom with shower and bidet and of course, the balcony. Already I could picture myself sitting there, glass of wine in one hand, paintbrush in the other, surrounded by flowers and painting to my heart's delight.

'It was built two years ago,' explained the agent. 'It has electricity, water and telephone line connected. It is ready for you to move in. There is no parking but you are free to park next door in the neighbour's courtyard.'

I could hear my heart beating faster and faster. I could not find any faults with the property. I was so excited that I telephoned Jan straight away and told her everything all in one breath. She approved, so I began taking photographs, hundreds of them, from every conceivable angle. I felt exactly as David Bailey must have felt in the 60s – what joy!

I made an offer at the asking price and returned to England, very excited and clutching my photos to show to all my friends and family.

I waited to see if my offer had been accepted. December passed with no news of the yellow villa. Then most of January went by as well. Then the English winter got to me and I was back in hospital – more needles, more pain, more visitors and more flowers. I couldn't sleep. I was restless with thoughts of Spain. Was the dream of the yellow villa dead?

In February I managed to send an email to the estate agent, asking what had happened.

He told me a local person had offered more than the asking price.

'But if you would like to come to Spain, I have other properties to show you?'

But my heart was set on the yellow villa, its marble tiles, the nearby deserted beach and the mountain covered in wild almonds, pomegranates, mangoes and avocado pears. I wanted that villa. Nothing else would do and besides, I had been showing the photographs to all my friends.

I was heartbroken.

I made a little shed in my garden and started to paint flowers, comforting my sorrow and absorbing my thoughts in painting.

-3-
Found my Jerusalem

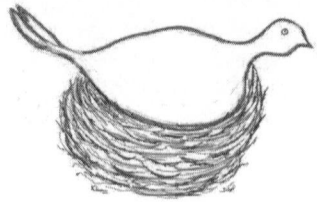

A little over a month later, I called the Spanish estate agent. He then casually mentioned that the buyer of the yellow villa had not been able to get a mortgage, so if I liked, I could put in another offer.

I wanted to jump with joy and shout at the agent, 'Why didn't you let me know? I only phoned by chance!' But I decided to play it calm and cool.

I pretended that I *might* be interested, as the villa did not meet my exact requirements. I moaned about it having no swimming pool or garage, that I had to walk through paddy fields to get to the beach and that the price was too high. I asked the agent if he thought the owner might lower the price.

The agent suggested that I return to Spain to see what could be done.

I knew I was not fit to fly, so I made the agent promise he would give me a couple of weeks and let me know immediately if anyone else put in another offer.

I could not get better fast enough. It was nearly four weeks before I got the go ahead from my doctor and was able to leave.

When I arrived in Spain, I realised everything was very mysterious. Sometimes I was told the villa owner was a she, at other times I was told the villa owner was a he who had gone to live in Malaga leaving his family to sell his home. I was beginning to wonder if it was a trap and not the property to buy after all.

Why was such a good property still on the market and why did the other buyer back out? Maybe not getting a mortgage was just an excuse…

Anyway, I negotiated a price, which was accepted. I paid a deposit and instructed a Spanish lawyer to go ahead with the exchange of contract – quickly.

-4-
Exchange of Contract

I was told the exchange of contract would take place on May 1st, so I went home to England to prepare myself. Jan and I decided to make a holiday of it, so we returned to Spain with the balance of the money in a banker's draft and two air mattresses, planning to stay in the villa after the exchange of contract.

We arrived in Malaga at 6pm. By the time we had collected our luggage and found the hire car office, it was past 8pm.

There was a long queue in the office, with many customers complaining about this and that. When we got to the front, it was gone 9pm, the charges were higher than we'd been told and the car we'd requested, with a roof rack, was not available.

All in all, a lot of hassle and we were happy to pull out of the car park at 10pm.

Driving along the motorway, both tired and hungry, I casually turned to Jan.

'Did you put my big red rucksack in the car?'

'No,' she said, then suddenly let out a scream, 'My handbag!'

In a sickening moment, we realised we had left the rucksack and the handbag, which contained our banker's draft, credit cards, cash wallet, villa purchase documents and our English house keys in the car hire office.

We could not get to the next exit of the motorway fast enough. All sorts of thoughts ran through our heads, I knew Jan was going completely doolally and I wasn't doing a rain dance either.

Would the car hire office be open when we got back? We couldn't even phone them because the mobile phones were in Jan's handbag too.

Our life savings and dream villa seemed a long way away in those long, tense moments. At the car hire office, Jan was out of the car before I'd even put the handbrake on. And there it all was, still on the pavement, next to where our car had been parked.

We were so happy that we forgot to discuss who was to blame. We reached our hotel in Calata at 1am, had dinner and wine and fell into bed, happy to have escaped the disaster of a lifetime.

The next day I took Jan to see the villa. We could only see the outside, but fortunately Jan loved it.

We set off to explore. Almayate is a working agricultural village. It has five bars and restaurants and one very large bodega – Lo Pepemolina – a place where villagers have their meetings, weddings and celebrations. It is also a place to settle arguments, in fact anything to do with village life starts there, and it serves excellent local food until 2 or 3am.

The village has a fruit and vegetable wholesale market, with deliveries going out to all over Spain. It has a school, a medical centre, and a church.

It is only 10 minutes away from a seaside town called Torre del Mar which means Tower of the Sea, or in English, The Lighthouse. Torre del Mar has a long promenade, a large marina and is near Calata, where we stayed. Calata is a very posh fishing village with a large marina that has a three-year waiting list for moorings for boats.

Further north is Torrox. The population is mostly German. Then further north again is Nerja, a town dominated by the English, which is famous for its caves that contain paintings by an ancient civilisation.

Nerja reminds me of Brighton without the pier, although it does have a breathtaking promenade called The Balcony of Europe.

The next day, Jan and I met the estate agent and lawyer and went along to the notary's office. The notary is the government's lawyer who oversees property transactions. There we got the shock of our lives – eleven people were waiting there, all of them, it seemed, involved in the transaction. It seemed that the whole village was selling the yellow villa.

We were all taken to one big consultation room and the seller's lawyer told us the banker's draft was not acceptable, probably because the family wanted the money in cash to avoid paying tax.

'And in any case,' he said. 'The price is now higher.'

Granada Town as seen from Alhambra Palace

Our lawyer told their lawyer that since the deposit had been accepted, the price could not change and that we could only pay with the banker's draft – take it or leave it.

There was a lot of arguing and kerfuffle in Spanish. Jan and I were partly terrified, partly bemused and totally silent.

Finally, the owners of the villa agreed to take our banker's draft on the condition that we go with them to the bank and cash it. We then realised that the bank was closed for two days. We protested that we were hoping to sign the contract and get the key so that we could spend the rest of our holiday in our new villa, so they agreed to let us have the key without any exchange of contract or cash. It was a bizarre situation but we didn't argue, we checked out of our hotel and headed for the villa, tired from the afternoon's ordeal of Spanish haggling, finger-pointing, shouting and arm wrestling. At the villa, our neighbours were waiting to greet us and we felt as if we became instant friends. They said they were distant relatives of the vendor but would not reveal the reason for sale (the mystery deepened!). Then we went for a stroll to Lo Pepemolina and had an excellent meal for the price of an English fry-up.

Strolling back from Lo Pepemolina, we saw a half-lit, half-open furniture shop, so we wandered in out of curiosity.

'Can I help you?' came a voice with a Birmingham accent.

We got chatting to the lady, and it turned out her father was a Pakistani from Lahore, where I am from originally – what a coincidence!

We made small talk, exchanged phone numbers and went off to our villa to sleep on our air mattresses, full of talk that the lady from Birmingham was surely a sign that we'd done the right thing.

In the middle of the night we were awake, very cold and very uncomfortable. The air had gone out of our mattresses and we were lying on the hard, marble flooring. Spirits slightly dampened, at dawn we set off for our hotel once more. I promised Jan a holiday in the Canary Islands as compensation.

After two days at the hotel, we returned to the notary's office. I could see my estate agent was nervous and my lawyer did not look very happy either. We all sat in the same room as two days previous and once again, the argument started about the price of the villa, with more finger-pointing, shouting and arm wrestling.

In the end, the village elder, called Antonio, said something loudly in Spanish and everybody went quiet and signed the documents. We exchanged the contract, I handed over the banker's draft, and all 11 people headed off to the bank to cash it. Afterwards, the lawyer, Jan and I went to a coffee bar to celebrate our ownership of the dream villa. Cheers!

-5-
The Yellow Villa

Jan and I returned to England as proud villa owners. I planned to return to Almayate as soon as I could, to start making myself at home there. In Canterbury, I bought a complete set of everything, from clothes to a new walking stick, so I would not have to carry everything to and from Spain.

I discovered my travel insurance would not permit me to stay in Spain for more than 45 days at a time, so I bought a return ticket for 40 days. Jan came with me for the weekend to help me carry my stuff, then she had to go back to work, so she left, leaving me to settle in.

The villa was in a charming little hamlet about a hundred yards from the rest of the village, with a small dirt track leading to the supermarket, café bar and high street.

The neighbours were charming too, all related to each other, and I was the only foreigner in their midst. Behind my villa, the lady was called Anna, her mother was called Anna and her grandmother was called Anna. As well as two sons, she had a daughter, also called Anna – quite imaginative, I thought. To be on the safe side, I called the mother Anna Senior and called the daughter Anna Bibi.

To the left of me was a builder living with his wife and elderly father. His wife was clearly related to Anna Senior but I never quite worked out how. To the right of me lived

Anna's sister and children. All in all, there were six houses around me.

The first thing I did after Jan left was make an onion bhajee , which I took to Anna Senior. After I introduced myself, she shared it round the village. Ever since, I had them eating from the palm of my hand.

I couldn't wait to start painting and I was amused to discover that art supplies in Spain were sold by house painters and decorators. There was no end of places to buy everything I needed. Really, I could not have asked for more.

I was also very impatient to create a garden in my little courtyard and on my balcony. I love flowers more than anything else I can think of, plus I wanted somewhere beautiful to sit and paint. So, I set off in search of a plant nursery or a garden centre.

Firstly I found a very large horticultural goods store. They sold tools, fertiliser, irrigation equipment, and decorated earthenware pots, some large enough to hide a person in (should you need to). In fact they had everything you could have ever wanted, but no plants.

The store manager only spoke a few words of English but he was very friendly. I spent hours in the store, looking at various strange objects I had never seen before. I asked so many questions that the poor chap got completely fed up with me, especially when I only spent four euros on some liquid plant feed when locals were waiting to order hundreds of euros worth of stuff for their market garden plots. But I used my charm and soon learned to ask questions when he wasn't busy, or I would capture him, then skulk away when rich customers arrived for service.

Eventually I discovered a proper plant shop behind the café in Almayate. The owner supplied local market gardeners with hundreds of fruit and vegetable plants, but he was also willing to sell a couple of dozen of anything to anyone he knew well. This was great news to my heart and I started stocking my garden and balcony with jasmine, hibiscus and bougainvillea.

It was around this time, that supermarket plastic bags began dominating my thoughts. I knew there was a bit of a crisis surrounding them in England. These hideous bags were out of control and threatening to engulf the country. I also read that Ireland had put a heavy tax on supermarket carrier bags to reduce litter in the countryside. I got quite fired up. I wanted to save the world from plastic bags!

You might ask what this had to do with plants. But I could see how combining the two could create a solution. Almayate was littered with plastic bags; whole streets were covered in them. They were hanging in the trees and drifting in the dry riverbeds. When the wind blew, they would fly towards your face like ghosts and zombies. In the Wild West, they had tumbleweed. In Almayate, we had plastic bags. It was ugly and hazardous, especially to wandering goats, sheep, cows and bulls that would sometimes swallow them and die.

I began my crusade of collecting all the plastic bags in the village. Anna Senior spread the news. I think the story went that Mad Professor Khan was doing a special experiment to get rid of plastic bags. It did not take long before I had thousands of bags and it was time to begin.

How could I make these bags multi-useful, instead of being used once to carry shopping then thrown away as litter? Firstly, I turned five bags into one, by lining them one inside the other, increasing their thickness and durability. Then I filled the bottom of the bags with strips of fabric and old newspapers. I loaded them into my Punto and took them to a building site where I filled them with topsoil and returned them to my patio garden. Then, by hand, I mixed peat into the soil and filled them with water from a watering can, waited until they had absorbed all the water, then filled them again. Now the bags were nice and rounded and firm. The rags and newspaper at the bottom acted as water storage for the plant's roots, perfect for survival in a hot climate and I planted seedlings of cherry tomatoes, lettuce, cress and aloe vera.

I used 100 supermarket plastic bags to make twenty compost bags. Can you imagine if everybody did that? How soon would all the bags disappear then! How about sending these bags to sub-Saharan Africa for people to grow their vegetable crops with very little water using all our plastic bags and rich country rags? No hard digging to be done and no weeds to manage either.

There is no fee for my expertise, so supermarket bosses please listen: collect all your used plastic bags, ship them to Africa and I will follow and do a plastic bag growing workshop for you, voluntarily. I am waiting for your telephone calls and emails.

After a time, I had bowls full of sweet cherry tomatoes from my experiment, but as well as this joy I also paid a heavy price. Filling the bags with soil and lifting them into the car boot was much too much for my unstable heart. I spent the next week in bed, howling with pain and wondering when the next heart attack would come. Anna Senior ticked me off severely and I have not yet told Jan of this stupid act of mine – how I would save the world from the curse of the carrier bag and save the starving in Africa. Now I cannot lift anything weighing more than two kilos.

I discovered another large garden centre just a few minutes away in the car. An English woman called Coral, her husband Wayne and son Rasheed lived nearby, so they came with me if I needed to lift bags of peat or large plants.

The first time I went there, I got completely carried away. There were hundreds of glorious bougainvilleas in all the colours of the rainbow, giant hibiscus in lipstick red, pink and white and jasmines bursting with little white flowers, rich in fragrance. It reminded me of my birthplace, an Indian village in Punjab. There, every evening a flower lady would come with a basket full of jasmine and, for a few pence would decorate my mother's earrings with jasmine buds. I still remember the aroma. The sight and scent of the jasmine was too much and I charmed one of the assistants to help me to collect several plants and deliver them to my villa. Seeing my stick and hearing about my heart problems, the dear soul did everything she could to help me, but she got into terrible trouble with her boss, who came round the corner and began screaming and waving his arms at her. I'm ashamed to admit I legged it . But sometime later, I met the boss in a café and explained about his kind-hearted staff. All is forgiven; it's surprising what the offer of a drink can do.

I was very restricted in what I could do in my garden, but I found people to help wherever I could. Wayne helped me re-pot my lemon, orange, frangipani, pomegranate and palm trees into larger pots when they outgrew their smaller ones.

I noticed there were many medicinal plants growing wild in Almayate. Sweet fennel, common thyme, lavender, rosemary, yarrow, aloe vera, castor oil, wild cherry, caper bush and camomile were just a few. I decided that the people of Spain needed them. The economy was booming, the rich settlers were coming from Western Europe and the poor immigrants were arriving from Eastern Europe and Africa. This left the Spaniards in the middle, making a mint, spending their money on the latest models of Chelsea tractors and converting their donkey sheds into villas with hot tubs. But it couldn't last forever, and when the economic miracle was over, the plants would offer a calming alternative to paella and spit-roasted pig. Spain was quietly providing what her people would eventually need.

Within a few weeks I realised I had to think seriously about my gardening expenditure. I imposed a strict rule on myself that I wasn't to spend more than fifty euros on plants on each visit to the villa. I still went to the garden centres to see the magnificent plants, but I walked away (mostly) empty-handed, consoling myself that I had no more room for them anyway.

-6-
My House Caretaker

Forty nights and days soon passed and I was due to catch the bus back to the airport. I felt very sad as I locked up the villa and caught the bus, and even worse when we passed the quiet beach and the calm, blue sea.

Anna Senior had come to wave me away and she promised faithfully to water my exotic flowers and plants that I loved so much. By this time, I had canna and calla lilies and jasmine trailing from the balcony and reaching the courtyard below where they entwined with deep purple bougainvilleas, a dozen hibiscus, oranges, tangerines, lemons and lemon verbena. I also had a pair of standard bay trees either side of the gate, looking like doormen and asparagus fern on the windowsill, twisting and turning, their luscious green a welcome relief for the eyes from the strong sunshine.

The plants in my planet-saving carrier bag pots would survive, but the exotic flowers in the earthenware pots would dry out quickly if they were not watered daily.

In the nearby fields, an automatic irrigation system was in place, taking care of cabbages and cauliflowers. The Moorish people established unique waterways here when they came from North Africa, making this region the garden of Spain. Alhambra Palace in Granada, created by the Moors, is the pride and joy of Spain. The Spanish tourist board says it is the biggest tourist attraction in the world after the Taj Mahal in India.

As well as my gardens, I needed someone to clean my house, so I put out some feelers in the village and found a nice lady who would do the job. Anna Senior got wind of this, stormed into my villa and told me in no uncertain terms that Anna Bibi would do the work and that she had told the other woman to go away.

Taking care of the garden was fine, but I really didn't really want Anna Senior interfering in my domestic life as I care for my privacy. But in Spain, your Spanish neighbours make friends with you and consider you one of their family. You have no privacy. So I had to either put up with it or move to a remote mountain villa and live like a hermit.

Sometimes, when I was up on the balcony painting, I would hear a commotion in the kitchen downstairs. It turned out that someone from next door had come in and switched the microwave on to make popcorn or warm their dinner. Other times they had begun a washing machine cycle to launder their own clothes. This, I was learning, was what it was like to have Spanish neighbours.

A sardine barbecue with friends

-7-
My Art in Spain

Back in England I longed for my yellow villa. It was as if I had enjoyed a holiday romance and was pining for my lost lover. I felt so liberated there, so artistic. Painting, art, creation and inspiration were the only things I had to think about there. In fact, sometimes my enthusiasm for the place threatened to tip me over into a happy madness.

Towards the end of August, I went back for more. I was not disappointed. One day, while strolling along the promenade at Torre del Mar, I saw some flamenco dancers busking.

One of them was so enchanting that my emotions began rushing through me like a speeding train. I wanted to stop the dancer in her tracks and capture her movements in a painting. I wanted to seize the movements of her hands, the curve of her body, the plumpness of her bosom, the strength of her neck, her strong thighs and the vibration along the ground of the click, click of her thunderous footwork. I loved that dancer and wanted to bottle her youth and passion. I sat there, sketching her for hours.

I always travel with a little satchel. It contains a sketchpad, charcoal, pens, pencils, some paints and brushes and a little bottle of water. Wendy gave this kit to me on my 65th birthday. Bless Wendy. She is such a sweet woman. She came to work for me in about 1982 when she was sweet 16. It was her first job and she packed herbal tea at my Herb Farm business in Canterbury. This tea went all over the world, to Harrods and Fortnum and Mason in London, to Macy's in New York and to Fauchon's in Paris.

Poor Wendy – packing all that tea. She was still working for me when I had to pack up in 2000 because of my heart problems. After that she went to work for my son and is still there now, filling perfume bottles.

In all those years Wendy never missed my birthday and always bought me a Christmas present. What devotion! Every time I open the satchel I remember her kindness and think of her like a daughter. Then I reach for the pad and start sketching whatever it is that caught my attention. I get so absorbed that I usually forget to eat or drink and end up either dehydrated or on the verge of a diabetic coma.

A week later, I took a trip to Barcelona to see my eldest daughter Sultana and my grandsons Yousuf and Seth, who lived there.

They lived near Gaudi's uncompleted inside-out cathedral, a masterpiece of unique architecture. Barcelona is such a magical city, full of vibration and excitement.

While I was there, I took time to sit in front of the cathedral, admiring the stone sculptures of doves that cascade down the spiral of the cathedral gate. The whole building was heavenly, like a fantasy world. It inspired me so much that I could not help getting my pad out. I started to sketch and then paint, page after page, Van Gogh style, with brush strokes of curvy, twisted, spiral lines, hoping to capture the cathedral's tower, each painting placed on the pavement to dry. I was so absorbed that I did not notice some Japanese tourists who had begun filming my activities and leaving me a pile of coins and notes. This was the first time I earned some easy loot from my art and of course, these masterpieces are now hanging in my daughter's flat.

When I got back to Almayate, I walked down to the sea. I had discovered a little hamlet the fishermen had constructed on the beach there. Each of the dwellings was unique, a higgledy-piggledy house made with stones, bricks and bamboo, reflecting the character of the inhabitants and beautified with bougainvilleas, jasmine, hibiscus, cactuses and palm trees.

One of the residents was called Paco. He was very artistic and had decorated his dwelling with a collection of things washed up out of the sea. He also had the most beautiful Bonsai plant collection dotted all over his courtyard beneath fig trees in which were swinging artist's sculptures and wind charms. Paco served coffee and sometimes freshly caught sardines from his little home. It was one of my favourite places to rest and make small talk in broken Spanish. My Spanish was made more broken by a drop or two of Paco's wine.

That day, as I walked past Paco's house, I noticed another house with line of giant dancing sunflowers in the garden of the house next door. They were swinging their heads in the air, like children chanting 'come and play', except I could hear them calling 'come and paint me!'

Sunflowers have always fascinated me and as I stood there dithering, I noticed the lady of the house stood in the doorway. I asked her if I could paint her sunflowers and she obliged me with a glorious bunch and a smile. I carried them to my villa with joy and spent the next three weeks sitting on my balcony painting them.

The pictures resulted in an exhibition called Sunflowers of Spain at the Gulbenkian Theatre Art Gallery, back home in Canterbury, Kent. The pictures were sold in aid of Seeds for Africa, a charity I support in Kenya, which feeds schoolchildren there. I thought it was strange and wonderful that a kind fisherman's wife on Almayate beach had helped those children in Kenya.

It was during that sunflower painting frenzy that I came up with the concept of Buzz Art.

The bodega in Almayate had installed a life size bronze sculpture of a fighting bull and it became quite an attraction for everybody. Children liked to swing from the bull's curvy tail and see how many of their friends they could seat on his back.

Everybody took photographs there. I even saw a young lady place some of her clothes on the bull's horns, then lay down on the floor with her legs high up in the air, playing dead, while her boyfriend took a picture.

Although I hated the idea of the fighting bull, I was as mesmerised as everyone else was by the statue. The sculptor had captured his power and muscles very well. He looked very angry to me, head down, his strong sharp horns ready to lash out at anyone that came his way.

I could not resist sketching the bull and as I was doing so, an idea began to form in my mind. It was a theory, that when we study something it causes little sparks in the brain as we understand what we are seeing, lighting up the mind. Each spark forms dots and lines, hence the picture you see: Buzz Art.

I was so excited by the development of this type of art that I did about 50 paintings in it. The beauty of it was that I didn't need to lug large canvasses around the countryside. A biro and paper was all I needed, then when the sketch was complete, I scanned it and printed it out as large as I liked. I hoped that one day, Khan's funky Buzz Art would be as popular as Picasso.

There was suddenly so much to sketch and paint that I easily became quite exhausted.

All the rooms in my yellow villa were filled with canvasses and all my best clothes were covered in blobs of paint. I didn't even care if I got invited out. I just went in my blobby clothes. Painting kept me happy and kept my mind from other things.

I travelled all over with my paraphernalia, village to village, mountain to mountain, field to field and beach to beach. I investigated flowers and trees, smelling their fragrance and tasting their fruits. 'Hola', I would say to them all. I was enjoying life and every second was a blessing to me.

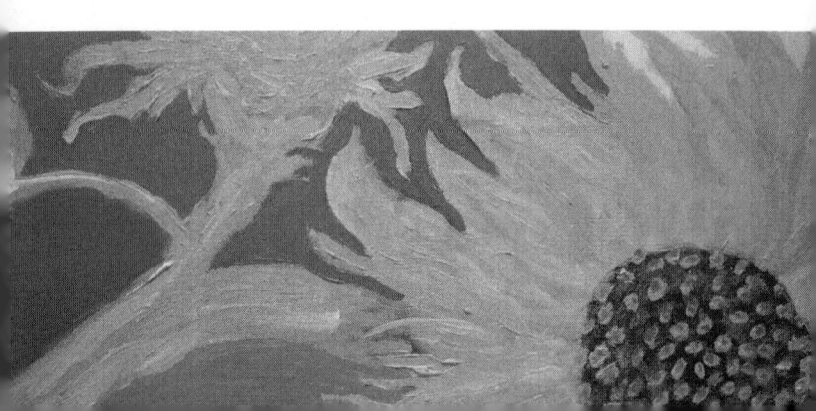

-8-
The Bruce Forsyth Tea Saga

Talking of Wendy, who bought me my artist's satchel, I remember one day, at the Herb Farm, when I was out of the office and she kindly answered my ringing phone.

'Hello, Herb Farm, can I help you?' she said.

'Bruce here,' came the reply.

'Bruce who?' said Wendy.

'Bruce Forsyth. Could you urgently send a few packets of your rosemary tea to my home address?'

'Yes, certainly Mr Forsyth!' She said sarcastically. 'Pull the other one , you can't fool me!' And she put the phone down.

Then I returned to the office.

'I hope it's okay,' said Wendy, 'but your phone was ringing, so I answered it. It was some joker calling, pretending to be Bruce Forsyth and asking for some rosemary tea. I told him to pull the other one and put the phone down. I hope I did the right thing.'

I was just about to answer Wendy when the phone rang again.

'Hello?' I said.

'Oh, good afternoon, Mr Khan. It's Mrs Mann, the buyer from Harrods' health-food department here. We've sold out of your rosemary tea and our best customer, Bruce Forsyth, urgently needs some. Could you send him some please? It's the only thing he'll drink to calm his nerves before he goes on stage.'

'Certainly,' I told her. Then I got off the phone and told Wendy to get some tea over to Mr Forsyth sharpish.

By this point, she needed a few cups for her own nerves!

The Village Almayate

There was always a lot of delivering taking place in Almayate. There were plenty of families in need of gas bottles, meat, bread and fish. In fact the fish man often came round with a bucket containing live squid and shellfish.

Also, there was often unbearable motorbike noise from the young people racing about. Occasionally I was woken by them in the middle of the night and wanted to throttle the lot of them. I am sure I was not alone in my plans.

I was not surprised that the whole area around Almayate was being developed at a rather alarming rate. Houses were appearing on the hills like mushrooms, especially those being built for tourists as holiday and retirement homes. They came, like me, for the year-round sunshine and winter temperatures of 18 to 20ºC. There was also the cheap, fresh food to consider.

I met many people of different nationalities, more and more of them came as bargain air flights increased. Some stayed near the airport and some were lured away to Torremolinos and Marbella, just 45 minutes away by car.
Five minutes away by car from Almayate was Niza beach. There you were allowed to camp overnight. Holidaymakers, both Spanish and other nationalities would put up their tents and sit, cooking paella over an open fire on the beach, enjoying the sea breeze.

Bulls still ploughed the fields to the east of the village. It was like a magical scene from medieval times and overlooking them on a high hill, was a very large, black statue of a bull.

It had once housed the adverts of an alcohol company and when the company folded, the council wanted to remove the bull. But the landmark was so popular that everyone protested. The bull's image could be seen everywhere after that – on cars, vans and trucks and bullock carts. The village was divided into upper and lower Almayate and had a seasonal stream running through it. The elders told me that once the only access to the village was through the stream's bed, pulled by bullock cart. The stream then became a road, which was lined with trees and beautiful wrought iron benches, where people sat to admire the Bull on the Hill.

The village also had a post office. A motorbike and an old banger of a car were parked outside, and the post was sorted on the pavement and stored in the banger. The postman would go off delivering on his 20-year-old motorbike. How he kept his balance, I could not work out. He wore no uniform but his bags carried a royal insignia. He did not deliver door to door, but stood at fixed spots across the village at certain times. People went to him to collect their mail and the mail of their neighbours. If you didn't have good relationships with your neighbours, you got no post. I never actually found out who brought my post.

-10-
The Dodgy Estate Agent

You may remember, when talk of dream villas was banned in our house and I was forced to go to Spain alone, that I spent a day looking for an estate agent.

While I was looking, I came across a shop window plastered with hand written notices about bargain properties. I told myself to keep away but curiosity got the better of me and after passing several times, I parked and went in.

Antonio greeted me like an old friend. He didn't ask me what I was looking for, he just took me to his car and off we went. I tried to talk to him about what I was looking for, but as he showed me rubble pile after rubble pile and countless animal sheds, I realised I wasn't getting through.

Everywhere I went with Antonio, he got a resounding welcome from the locals. He knew everyone. It seemed he had helped many of them with their property and they all wanted to buy him coffee and tapas and meet his new friend – me. I was impressed by his popularity. He spoke a little English, German and French and Italian. He was in his 30s. He was tall, handsome and walked like a stallion, full of confidence and conviction.

In the late afternoon, Antonio took me to the mountains to show me a 'fantastic bargain'. 'Many metres with almond and avocado trees and a fantastic view of the sea,' he said.

'The owner is very old man. He wants to move into a town flat near his son. Offer any price. I will do the document free for you. You are my friend, I want to help you.'

As Antonio was explaining all this to me I didn't dare to disagree. I was worried about where we were going, but even more worried about his driving on the unstable, hilly, dirt tracks. The hillside was littered with the skeletons of cars, jeeps and vans that had slipped over the edge. As he drove, Antonio was smoking and also making and receiving calls on his mobile phone. Antonio kept pointing out a small white dot to me. 'That is the finca,' he said. But we could not find our way to it. Antonio was getting mad and a little embarrassed. I asked him if he had any details about the property or a map. He pointed to his head. 'All details here,' he said.

It was beginning to get dark, so I politely suggested that we try again in the morning. I didn't dare to tell him that I couldn't live up a hill, as I cannot climb more than a dozen stairs without fighting for breath. He agreed and we went back to the office, where I breathed a sigh of relief. We shook hands, said goodbye and agreed to meet in the morning. I never went there again.

One day, after I bought my villa, I passed his shop again. It was boarded up. I enquired in the café next door and they told me Antonio had 'gone away' and the shop would not be opening again.

-11-
Breakfast with Figs

August in Almayate was the season of plenty. Wherever you went, trees were laden with fruit. Mangoes dangled from the trees like monkeys. Also hanging from the branches were purple-reddish balls – delicious, mouth-watering pomegranates – the favourite fruits of the Arabs who brought them from Morocco to Andalucia. Have you ever tasted fresh pomegranate juice? It is delicious – sweet and tangy. Then there were the sweet, juicy plums – green, purple and gold. Not to forget the cooling flesh of the watermelons, one will do for the whole family.

I had a friend who went to the market, bought about one hundred watermelons, put them in his Land Rover, and went off to the beach and sold them. It only took him an hour to sell the lot and make a couple of hundred euros. People buried them in the sand near the seashore to make them cool and ideal for quenching thirst. They cooled in half an hour and were eaten in five minutes.

My first August in Almayate, I was busy trying to paint the morning glory flower. I had grown them from seed and was most surprised when they bloomed in all the colours of the rainbow. I couldn't resist growing them all over the balcony and there they dangled in blues, pinks, reds and whites. I loved how their cheerful little trumpets greeted me in the morning. It always lifted my spirits.

To paint them I had to get up at 6am to prepare. They opened their petals at about 6.30am before the sun got too strong, and they closed again a few hours later.

I began by priming the canvas. Then I sketched as many as possible before spending the morning painting.

At 11am, exhausted and ready for breakfast, I dawdled to the bodega for coffee con leche and a tapas omelette. I ate them outside on the patio looking at the mountains on one side and the Mediterranean on the other.

By the patio were orchards of avocado pears, multicoloured bougainvillea and palm trees. After breakfast I wandered down and sat under the fig trees, looking for the fattest ones to eat. They made the most delicious dessert after breakfast and tasted even better because they were free. I ate a bellyful, then collected a few more and wandered back to the balcony. I finished painting the morning glory then got ready for lunch, with more figs for pudding.

The Moorish village of Frigiliana

-12-
The Honest Estate Agent

There were two estate agents in Almayate. One was owned by a woman from Majorca. I called her Anna-Maria. She was full of life — completely mad in any business sense, but very, very honest. She had very artistic tastes and in her shop window, among the properties for sale, were wonderful displays of agricultural tools and artefacts collected from old ruins and fincas – also for sale. It was the most imaginative estate agent window display I have ever seen.

Anna-Maria had a large, open-plan office full of computers she didn't understand, filing cabinets and a round table, always full of seasonal fruits and flowers. She spoke very fast and rushed about, never sitting down, always busy like a bumblebee buzzing about. She buzzed around clients bombarding them with information.

As I said she was honest and many times I heard her say: 'Don't buy that property. It has family disputes and lots of claims that would take years to settle. It is only a good bargain if you like to gamble. I can recommend a lawyer.'

Anna-Maria also managed rental properties, which were her real income. I doubted she ever made money from selling property. Germans liked to rent a local property for six months, get a feel of the area, then if they liked it, continued to rent while they built their dream property. It was a very sensible idea. I heard many horror stories about English people who would sell everything they had in the UK, move to Spain lock, stock and barrel, ending up with no property, no job, and nothing to go back to when things did not work out.

I liked Anna-Maria, and as her shop was only three hundred yards from my home, I would often go there for a chat with the help of a Spanish dictionary. I would go next door first, to the café, and buy a coffee con leche for Anna-Maria and tea for myself then settle in for a very amusing hour or two.

Sometimes Anna-Maria would let me put one of my paintings in her window. Lots of interest but no sales, unfortunately. Anna-Maria was always finding attractive, educated assistants to work in her shop, but they never stayed long. Perhaps they could not stand her bumblebee style.

Anna-Maria had a lawyer who came from Malaga by bus two or three times a week. He was an exceptionally handsome young man, very polite and spoke good English. He was very puzzled about how English lawyers managed to charge their clients for thinking time. We had many laughs about it. English lawyers take people to the cleaners with their charges. In Spain there are fixed charges for certain legal transactions. He envied the rich English lawyers and their outstanding charges.

One day I saw a villa in Anna-Maria's window I liked the look of. It was built on a hilltop with gorgeous sea views, surrounded by mango groves and a secure fence. It had a swimming pool, modern architectural design, and a Moorish courtyard complete with fountain and double garage. Inside were four big bedrooms, a drawing room with dark wood beams and an open fire, a porthole window overlooking the sea and all mod cons. It was absolutely out of this world and I planned to buy it and rent it out to hikers. I asked Anna-Maria how much it was. She said it was a bargain as it belonged to a German who would accept a good price because he had already returned home to Germany.

'I will tell you price. See it first,' she said. 'Few miles, near here, just ten minutes drive.'

So we set off in her four-wheel drive. Nearly an hour later we were there, having crossed several small rivers on the way. At some points I did not think we would make it and I began to wonder what I was doing – diabetic, with heart, back and stomach problems – if I had chest pains or fell into a diabetic coma here, only the Spanish vultures would have found me.

All that was forgotten though when we arrived at the villa on the hill and made our way up the drive. There were trees everywhere and they were lush with pomegranates, avocado pears and mangoes the size of small melons, red and yellow, ready to be squeezed into your mouth. My heart began to pump with joy. Anna-Maria asked me if I wanted some mangoes. 'Not half!' I said and I was out the car, filling my rucksack. When that was full, I piled them onto the back seat and across the dashboard.

As we reached the villa I was stunned by how beautiful it was. I started taking photographs in every direction.

'I must have this villa,' I said to Anna-Maria. 'Hikers will love it!' Adding under my breath, 'And I can keep the mangoes, pomegranates and avocado orchards for myself.' Anna-Maria told me the price in however many millions of pesetas. I worked out that it was about 50,000 euros.

'Are you sure Anna?' I said. 'Yes,' she replied, 'and maybe you can put in lower offer'.

'It's not possible,' I replied. 'Are you sure and sure and sure? Because if you are I will give you a cheque right now for the whole amount.'

Anna-Maria insisted. Back at the office her English-speaking lawyer friend checked the price of the villa on the computer. It was 500,000 euros. Anna-Maria had put the decimal point in the wrong place in her mind. I had to go home and comfort my soul with the juicy mangoes of Almayate.

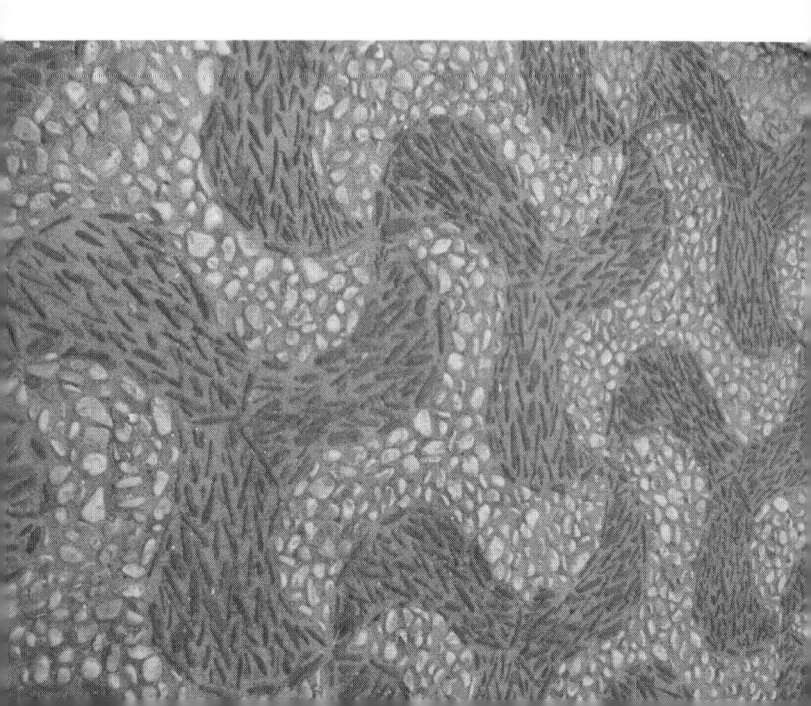

Human Fog in the Supermarket

In Almayate, smoking was the number one pastime. They considered it their human right to have this pleasure. I was sure the residents even smoked in their sleep. As a consequence, I could smell a constant, horrible tobacco aroma for miles around my villa. As I walked around, people greeted me with 'Hola!' and at the same time they would be blowing tobacco smoke in my face. And as I ate my grilled squid, chips and a glass of tinto in the bodega, I was aware of a constant fog covering my food.

One day I was in a supermarket, which sells fresh bread, fresh meat, fresh fruit and fresh vegetables. I was at the butcher's counter buying a lovely free-range chicken, when I smelt a funny smell. Guess what? An old man was walking around the supermarket and he was smoking a big, fat cigar that was blowing smoke everywhere. I could not believe it. There he was, fiddling with fresh bread as he smoked all over it. The butcher became so fog-bound that I dropped everything there and left. There were "No Smoking" signs in the supermarket but nobody took any notice. It is simply a formality of the EU and the local health regulations.

No one cares. I was told firmly that if I wanted to protest, I should go ahead and prepare to have no friends in the village. I decided to chicken out, suffer in private and be happy.

Traditional Sherry Tasting

The Almayate Paella Festival

-14-
Daily Chores

I developed a routine in Almayate. They were happy days that revolved around my plants and painting, exploring for the former and seeking inspiration for the latter.

I got up at around 9am and opened the bedroom shutters to see the sea, the sandy beach, palm trees, blue skies, and birds. The sun was usually so strong that I had to put my hand to my forehead. I could see my plants spread out before me like an oriental carpet. I would stand there for about half an hour, hoping to spot dolphins, but it only happened once or twice a year when they were on their migratory route.

I would then go downstairs and make myself the first cuppa of the day in a large mug. Then I would prepare toast, cereal and fresh fruit including melons, mangoes, peaches, oranges – all of which I would put on a tray and bring up to the balcony, very slowly.

Sitting there, I would sip my tea, nibble my breakfast and learn some new Spanish words. It seemed to me that I only had room for a certain amount of Spanish words in my brain. Any new ones I learned replaced the ones I already knew, which were quickly forgotten, but I carried on in hope.

I would then pace about on the balcony, shouting a few 'Buenos Dias's to passing neighbours, take a shower, take my medicines and begin painting whatever was on the upstairs easel.

Then at 1pm, I would prepare a quick lunch and glass of tinto, which I would enjoy on the balcony before going to the café for coffee to meet locals for chitchat. Home then for siesta until 5pm, after which I would have another shower, water the garden, drink tea while admiring the plants, then wander through the paddy fields to the beach to fish until about 9pm.

I'd come home and watch a little TV. Then, if I were too tired to cook, I would wander to the bodega for steak, chips and tinto. If I met friends, I would perhaps stay there until 2 or 3am, then stagger slowly home to bed.

This was the usual pattern but some days I didn't feel like doing anything at all.

Other days I would drive into the mountains to take photographs of the local fauna and flora, eat a packed lunch, do some sketches or pop to the garden centre and go home, full of ideas.

Then I would get my sketchpad and prepare for painting, sometimes until midnight, eating only sandwiches before bedtime.

Occasionally I would get up, go to the café for a cheese roll and coffee and head for the beach. I'd take a chair, a beach mat, a bottle of water, some fresh fruit, bait from the freezer and a notebook and pen. Then I would spend the whole day, throwing the line into the water and dreaming, writing, fishing, and bathing, but mainly dreaming.

About a mile away down the beach from where I usually sat, was a nudist sunbathing club. That first August, when I had some guests visiting from England, they strolled down there. They were thirsty and asked for a drink and were told they'd be most welcome, if they were naked.

I don't know what they did with their clothes but they came back quite exhilarated and told me about their pleasant nude experience. I think they are now looking for a mobile home so they can join the club permanently. I have yet to gather the courage to undertake this particular adventure myself, but I've been dreaming about it for years.

-15-
Tonbridge Station

Going to and from Spain always involved a trip via Kent's Tonbridge station. I would catch the train from Canterbury West, near my house, having prepared everything the day before with a list that I double-checked as I packed.

I had to be very careful not to overload myself, as that would be suicidal. I simply couldn't carry more than five kilos at the most, due to my delicate condition.

Most important were my passport, credit cards, Spanish chequebook, medicines and medical insurance certificate. Next I packed a diary of important telephone numbers, the digital camera, mobile phone charger, toiletries, gifts for Anna Senior, and the key for the yellow villa.

For the journey I needed a bottle of water, sandwiches and glucose tablets, nitro-glycerine spray for possible heart emergencies, pens, sketchpad and a notebook. All this added up. It was packed into my satchel and a case on wheels.

Tonbridge is a dirty, miserable Victorian station. I don't think it has been painted or cleaned since it was built. It has no soul and the first time I went I nearly killed myself dragging my case up several flights of stairs to change platforms. That was before I noticed the lift. There were no signs, I think they hid it on purpose so they could watch me on the CCTV for their own amusement. I never found anyone to help me at Tonbridge station. As far as I was concerned it was hell on earth.

-16-
Gluing up the Passport

In September, I flew to Spain. I arrived at the internet ticket collection desk and was concerned to see a long line of travellers. I only had an hour before my flight. I discovered that some tickets had not arrived in time so the solo receptionist was writing each one out by hand. She was also answering the phone, pacifying someone who sounded quite angry.

Finally I collected my ticket and went to check-in. I answered the security questions, then handed over my ticket and passport.

'I'm sorry Sir,' she said. 'We cannot take you on this passport. It's falling to pieces.'

I was stunned. I'd never heard of this being an issue.

I paused. 'Well I travel a lot,' I said, 'please can I go?'

'No Sir, I'm afraid not. I can ring my supervisor to explain it to you if you like.'

'Yes, please,' I said, not quite panicking yet.

I waited for a long time. Not surprisingly people behind me were becoming very agitated. Then the supervisor came and examined my passport.

'Sorry Sir, I cannot allow you to fly to Malaga on this passport. It's in tatters.'

I began to wish an enormous hole would appear and swallow me up. I felt a right plonker, but I decided it was best to keep calm. I thanked him, took my passport, left the queue, went to WHSmith, bought a tube of UHU glue and made my way to McDonald's. I quickly glued my passport back together, taking care not to stick my hand to it. Then I went to the bathroom and held it under the dryers until it looked vaguely normal. Then I made my way back to the Malaga check-in counter, avoided eye contact and sailed through, vowing as I collected my boarding card that on my next trip home I would apply for a new passport.

-17-
Karen and Miriam's Success

Almayate had an interesting warehouse of domestic appliances that was run by two local ladies, Karen and Miriam. There was no window to display goods. Inside was an 'office', just a telephone and table surrounded by washing machines, freezers, microwaves, dishwashers, cookers and fridges. They were all slightly damaged, dented or chipped, but in perfect working order with the normal manufacturers' guarantee. They were brand new from the maker's factory but about 30% cheaper than the recommended price because each piece had been slightly damaged in transit between the factory and distribution points. The distributors write them off as an insurance loss but the manufacturers still offered a guarantee for full parts and repairs.

Every time I went past the warehouse it was full and the two ladies were making so much of a killing that they were thinking about opening another branch.

Karen spoke German and English. She'd been working in an estate agent's but found the hours too long and the commission too low. She needed to earn good money to look after her diabetic child. She met Miriam at the school gate. Miriam was also dissatisfied with her lifestyle. Her husband had a warehouse that he didn't know how to use and together they hatched the plan.

In Spain, cheap was the name of the game when it came to selling goods. They got a 5,000 Euro grant to start a business and one year's free rent from Miriam's husband. Three or four times a week Karen went to Malaga to collect the stock in their van, meanwhile Miriam stayed in the shop, taking cash only and orders with cash deposits.

In the mornings they took their children to school and at around 9am, came to the Maria café in Almayate for breakfast at 9.30am and opened the warehouse at 10am. Sometimes I met Karen and Miriam in Maria's café for breakfast and to hear the village gossip. At 2pm they closed the warehouse, collected their children from school and went home for a siesta, returning to the shop at 6pm, opening until 9pm and so their routine continued until Friday. Weekends were for taking the family to the beach.

I watched Karen and Miriam with fascination, observing how their lifestyle, clothing and appearance changed, as they became more affluent. When I last returned from England I was greeted with the news that Karen had left her husband to concentrate on building up the business. Poor chap.

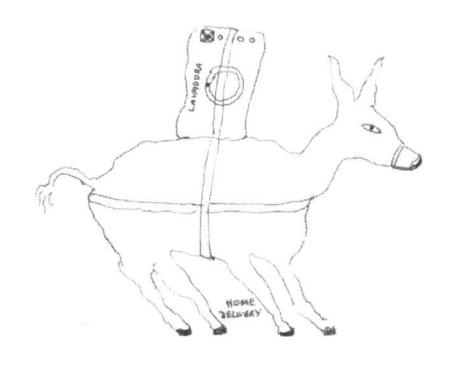

-18-
The Tony and Sheila Fiasco

As well as the washing machine warehouse, Almayate had a very interesting bric-a-brac shop containing Moorish bazaar rugs, carpets, wooden carvings, wooden tables, brass tables, and mirrors. Tony and Sheila ran it. They had a daughter called Sophia who was about 13 years old.

I got to know Tony and Sophia when they told me their heart-breaking story of making their life in Spain. They came from Newcastle. Tony was Moroccan but brought up in an English care home. He was a bit of a rascal in his school days and met Sheila who was working for social services. She was half Chinese, with a father from Hong Kong and a mother from Newcastle, where they ran a Chinese takeaway together.

Sheila met Tony, and they dated for a short while and got married without her parent's blessing. They eloped to Walsall where they did market trading, odd jobs and car repairs. Then they had a baby. Life was a struggle for Tony and Sheila.

Then one day, Tony saw an advert for a cheap holiday to Spain – Torremolinos, all in, £199 – what a bargain. He booked it as a surprise for his wife and the baby and they fell in love with Spain. The relaxed atmosphere, cheap food, sunshine, street markets and Moorish culture all appealed.

They went back to England, sold their flat and returned to Torremolinos where they bought a small flat while they looked for somewhere bigger to buy and a business opportunity. It wasn't long before they bought an old Jeep, a two-bedroom flat and met a market trader who showed an interest in Moroccan goods. He told Tony that if he imported a 20ft container of Moroccan goods, he would be willing to buy them for his Sunday market stall. Sheila and Tony were so excited, imagining how they would import thousands of tonnes of Moorish goods and sell them all over Spain. Tony still had some family connections in Morocco so he travelled to Tangier and bought enough stuff to fill a 40ft container. Sheila and Tony had to sell their flat and move into rented accommodation to pay for the 40ft container, the goods, shipping costs and custom duty. But when the goods arrived the buyer was nowhere to be found and the markets were full of Moorish items much cheaper than those Tony had bought in Tangiers.

Tony tried selling wherever he could, but he soon discovered the business was 'covered' and he was told he'd better clear out or get his legs chopped off.

Tony and Sheila had nowhere to keep their stock but they managed to rent a tiny shop and tried to sell from there. Eventually they ran out of cash, couldn't afford to rent their flat and had to live in the back of their shop with a makeshift kitchen and bathroom.

It was a dreadful life and began to affect their daughter Sophia at school. I could also see their relationship was starting to be affected. Sheila would come to my villa, make tea and small talk, then dissolve into tears and explode with anxiety and fear about their uncertain future and Sophia's changing behaviour at school, about which the teachers were complaining. I tried to give Sheila advice and let her use my bathroom to take a shower and refresh herself. Then she'd have more tea and go back to the shop.

A few days later, Tony would come to the villa and repeated the whole episode. I gave them my best advice. I told them to offer the stock to a local wholesaler in Malaga at half the price so they could recover at least 50 per cent of their savings, rather than lose all of it.

During the conversation I discovered that Tony was very good at electrical work. He helped me around the villa and did a good job fixing all the electrics and doing other small jobs like hanging a chandelier and sourcing a new kitchen for me.

I then advised him to advertise his services as a handyman and removal service, as he still had a large van. Tony didn't follow any of my advice. Then I went to England, but when I returned found out Sheila was three months pregnant. By then, most of the stock had been sold, Tony was suddenly doing very nicely as a handyman, Sophia was making progress at her new school and Tony and Sheila's relationship was back on a loving footing.

By then Tony and Sheila were renting a two-bedroom flat at Torre del Mar and trying hard to get rid of their Moorish goods at the local market. The baby arrived, a little girl, and very nice it was too. A cuddly little baby, who hardly made any noise, just slept, sucked her mummy's milk and went back to sleep.

But then disaster struck them again. Their landlord wanted them out so he could make double the normal rent from tourists over the summer. Sheila had not signed any sort of agreement with the landlord, so they had no leg to stand on. It was very difficult to find rented accommodation at that time of year, what with holiday bookings pouring in. Over summer, the population in Torre del Mar swells from 15,000 to 45,000 and you can find people sleeping anywhere and everywhere, from balconies to beaches.

I suggested they go and see a friend of mine known as Kind Boat Lady. And as the story went, she rented them her place in Almayate for one month – a temporary reprieve.

After that, Sheila found a villa near my place in Almayate. It had four walls, a door, a window, a toilet and shower, an incomplete floor and a space for Tony's workshop. It did once belong to an Englishman who was building a dream villa for his own retirement, but in the process of building it he passed away, so his trustees wanted a quick sale. Tony and Sheila bought it. How they managed to find the deposit and get a mortgage, I didn't dare ask. But I was so pleased that after five years of struggling, Tony had a home for his family.

-19-
There's One Born Every Minute

It is incredible, with all the publicity and news about crooked and dodgy house selling and buying in Spain, that some people are not aware of any of the pitfalls.

You'd think they would know it all by heart, but not according to this hair-curling and heart-breaking saga.

There was a lovely, blonde, attractive businesswoman, Jane, from Glasgow. She had been looking for her dream house in Spain for four years. Someone had offered to buy her Scottish cleaning business and she thought it was the perfect time to sell up and go abroad.

She went to a Spanish property dealer in Glasgow, where she saw many properties for sale in his window, and off she went.

In Spain, she saw many newly constructed houses, but there was always something she didn't like. Either she liked the property and not the area or liked the area and couldn't find a desirable property and so on and so on.

She had some relatives in Torremolinos where she had many happy holidays while seeking her dream home, but she couldn't stay there permanently as she had dogs and cats and horses that needed room.

She wanted something special, near the sea and in the country, where she could take the dogs on the beach while riding her horses. Jane needed plenty of space to have stables. But she still wanted to be near civilisation because she wanted her elderly mother to live with her and so needed to be close to the local doctors, supermarkets and all other civilised necessities such as restaurants and café bars.

One day, when she was passing her local estate agent's window, she saw a notice for a plot of land where a dream house of her own design could be built. The village was near the sea and five minutes walking distance from all restaurants, café bars, supermarkets and doctors. There was plenty of room for her stable and horses, too.

The advert said an experienced builder could build your dream home in six months. It promised an architect-designed house, all travel organised, meetings with the local architect, and experienced builders and developers included.

Best of all, the land was only 60,000 Euros and building a house would cost 80,000 Euros.

Jane just could not resist this offer. She thought it was too good to be true.

'Hurrah!' she thought, 'my ship has come in. No more cold, wet, rainy Glasgow. My mother will be warm and comfortable, with all day sunshine and respite from her aches and pains, arthritis and rheumatism. Jane dreamt about riding on the lonely beach with her dogs, having country walks amongst almond blossom, peaches, mango groves and olive trees – let's go!'

Arriving with her mother, Jane saw the plot of land for the first time. It was 15 metres wide and a couple of hundred metres long, narrow, and stretched between two country cottages, with olive, fig and pomegranate trees on one side and the sea on the other.

In the fields where her dream home would one day stand, Jane could see fields of tomatoes and globe artichokes, the shimmering refection of the sea and, at the back of this little hamlet, mountains and valleys, lush with oranges, lemons and avocados.

Garden after garden made a criss-cross pattern over the hills like patchwork on a quilt. Different shades of greens and blues made it heart-warming and there was a little stream passing by where the local boys caught tadpoles.

Jane was told this plot was highly desirable, a real bargain. The cost of a garage in Edinburgh! She went to the developer's lawyer, signed over €60,000 for the land and €40,000, half the deposit of the house, to the builder – a final cost of €140,000 and went for a grand celebration dinner with her mother at the local restaurant.

Six months down the line, Jane, back in Glasgow, with her house on the market, had kept in touch with the builder and architect who were creating her dream home. Unable to contain her excitement, she arranged a visit to Spain, to see the progress and daydream about her enormous house and new life.

When she arrived, there was nothing to be seen. The builder and architect explained they were waiting for planning permission, which wouldn't be a problem.

'As soon as the 'no objection' agreement comes from the neighbour and planning permission is granted, we'll be away,' the builder told Jane.

'By the way, can I have some more money for building materials. There's a construction boom and prices are going up so it's best I buy them now. It's for your benefit.'

By now Jane was a little suspicious, so she made some enquiries, starting with her new neighbours.

They had received no letter from the architect or the developer requesting the objection agreement. So she went to the council offices, where she was told planning permission had been applied for, but it was highly unlikely she would get it, because the council had plans to build a road on that very spot. It was an old abandoned railway track to Malaga, which was shut down in Franco's time.

Her options were to live in a mobile home, with her mother, horses and dogs or resell the plot at a higher price to the next Jane from Glasgow with the same desires and aspirations of wanting to live in Spain.

-20-
Green and Stripy Store

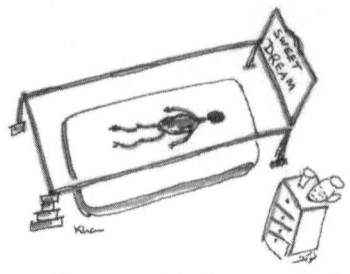

When I first moved to Spain, I needed to furnish the yellow villa. I was recommended a shop just outside Nerja, called Green and Stripy. It was a Spanish shop that specialised in house furniture, electrical appliances, kitchen and bathroom fittings, patio and garden goods. People flocked there from all over. If you had an empty house and wanted to fill it with furniture, then that was the place to go. It was so busy the staff didn't have time to breathe.

I went to the store with a list of everything I needed. I saw a cooker and asked if it had a fan in the oven. I was told yes, so I ordered it. Then I ordered three beds complete with mattresses and sommiers – metal frames. I bought chandeliers for two of the bedrooms and spotlights for the kitchen and bathroom. I bought a television and especially asked the salesman if it had the latest socket for my video camera and was told it had. I also bought a three-piece suite and dining table with chairs I liked. All in all, I spent about €6,000 and was quite pleased with myself.

Pleased that was, until my goods were delivered, when I discovered the oven didn't have a fan, the TV didn't have the socket I needed and the sommiers made a squeaking noise whenever you moved in bed.

So I went back to the store and very politely explained that a few of the goods I had bought were not what was promised and I was prepared to pay more money in exchange for better class of goods. They just told me to get lost.

I explained again: 'I am a good customer, I spent a lot of money here,' I said, but my appeal fell on deaf ears.

So I went to the town hall consumer affairs department, which after two days of being pushed from pillar to post, I found in the corner of another office.

I was told to go back to the store and collect a complaint form. I would have to fill it in, get the store to stamp it, then take it to the town hall to have my problem investigated.

Back at the store, the manager told me I would need all the receipts to collect the form. I gathered them together and with the aid of a Spanish dictionary, I filled in the form, made three copies and returned to the shop.

I decided to give the manager one more chance to upgrade my goods but he refused, so I went to the town hall and lodged my complaint form.

Pleased with myself, I waited and waited, until three months passed and I received a letter from the store's lawyer informing me that if I would go back to the store, they had a solution for my problem.

I appeared at the Green and Stripy in such a jubilant mood. I showed the letter to the manager, but he snatched it from my hand, threw it in the air and again told me to get lost. I was so humiliated.

I returned to the Town Hall where I was told that they had no legal power to do anything. All these European Union trading standards laws are complete rubbish, I thought.

My advice is whatever you buy in Spain, inspect it carefully, because you have no protection and the bureaucratic system is so laborious that it's not worth the hassle of trying to sort it out.

After a year I received a note saying I should go to the town hall to collect a letter telling me what had happened regarding my complaint. I never went. It would probably tell me I had been unsuccessful and that the store had been given a special award for its services to foreign customers.

-21-
Trip to The Rock

The following year, in April, the Nerja International Club were having their end of season trip to Gibraltar and invited me along. I had to leave at 6am to meet them at 7.40am. I didn't sleep a wink, worrying in case I missed my alarm. I was to meet them on a coach at a bus stop on the Algarrobo roundabout. A few other Brits would also be waiting.

It was very busy there at that time in the morning, with lots of workmen waiting to be picked up by their colleagues and traffic rushing past – a bit like Piccadilly Circus. Lots of roads came together there and high-rise flats surrounded the whole area.

I parked my car near what I thought was the right bus stop. There was no one else there and I started to get a bit worried. I walked around but I couldn't see any Brits anywhere. Then at 7.40am I saw a bus about half a mile away, flashing its lights. I waved my stick hoping to attract the driver's attention, then someone got off the bus and started frantically beckoning me. There was nothing to do but dash for it. Due to my heart condition and panic, I couldn't move very fast. I felt I was going to miss the bus. Palpitations started, getting faster and faster as my breath got heavier. But finally I made it and collapsed on the first seat I could see. I shouted 'sorry' as loudly as I could and the coach moved off.

The coach was full with thirty or forty Englishmen. I sat next to John from Celata. We exchanged our telephone numbers as you do when you meet strange Englishmen in foreign parts of the world. We started to have a conversation about the golf, English weather, mortgage and bank interest charges and how Spain has a good climate and cheap houses. You can sell your two up and two down terrace house in England and from the proceeds you can buy a place of your dreams here, and still have change to have couple of years of good golf. By the time your money runs out your house price has doubled, so you downgrade your luxury villa to campo casa and start all over again, a life of luxury, that was John's philosophy. I do not want to take responsibility here for this advice — if you do sell your house in England, rush down to Spain with your wife and children and things don't work out then don't blame me for it! After nearly two hours of nerve-racking coach journey and bullshit conversation we had our first glimpse of The Rock. I must say, I was impressed, it was standing upright, saying here I am, come and climb me. It is like Everest without the snow. I was surprised to see, how steep it is. Just like a giant whale coming out of the sea to take breath, you may be forgiven for thinking it might go down at any minute and disappear forever.

Gibraltar is the last frontier of British colonial rule and such ingenuity and expertise of engineering has gone into making it viable. It's the smallest colony in the English crown with Airport, shipping port, marina, supermarket, shops, pubs, Army barracks, and a shipyard.

A friend of mine, Dr Dorothy Price, who retired from England from an academic career settled in Nerja. She is an expert in Spanish history, and she tells me that during the Second World War, tunnels were dug in the Gibraltar rock so large that it can now accommodate 10,000 soldiers with all the military paraphernalia necessary to defend The Rock against any invasion at that time. The mind boggles, no wonder the film producers of that James Bond 007 movie took advantage of The Rock's height and used the hair-raisingly complicated twists and turns of the road going up The Rock to give us suspense in the film! Of course, Gibraltar has a cemetery for sailors who gave their lives for England. The most famous battle of Trafalgar was fought not far from The Rock and the body of Lord Nelson, English Naval Hero, was brought to Gibraltar after the victory in the battle and preserved here in the barrel of brandy before being sailed to England for a ceremonial burial as one of our greatest heroes of all time.

Every step you take at The Rock is full of history and interesting stories. The place has a magical atmosphere and is very nostalgic for English visitors, even Prince Charles came here first in the Royal Yacht for his honeymoon to fly the British Flag. When English visitors from Spain come here they go straight to the pub for warm English beer, roast beef and Yorkshire pudding, bacon butties, fish and chips. Then get drunk and go to the Supermarket, buy booze and cigarettes and those not so drunk venture out to climb The Rock by foot or by lift. When they reach at the top, they usually get robbed by the famous Gibraltar Apes, who steal their cameras, handbags, shoes, wallets or anything else that can be sold off at the monkey business club in exchange for a banana. Some have heartbroken stories and some scratches on their hands to show their battle of tug of war with the Apes trying to snatch their bags, but, at the end of the day, they have enjoyed it. They have a good outing and clear off happy as Larry to their villas in Spain until next time around. By the way, a compulsory sing-song in the coach on the way back is "Oh for he's a jolly good fellow", which always frightens the Spanish coach driver, I wonder why he just doesn't just leg it.

I was not able to go up The Rock and enjoy the view to die for or have the tug of war with the monkeys as my legs and heart refused to go any further, so I spent the afternoon reading names and ages of the soldiers in the cemetery. Boys who were so young when they died in the battle of Trafalgar, and I spent some time looking at the governor's house.

I was very lucky - within a few weeks after the trip to The Rock I was taken up in a light aircraft by a friend of mine, she is a very talented lady who wanted to be a millionaire, dealing in properties in Spain and Morocco, and before that she was a guru in high finance in the city. She is a very good pilot and takes her property clients to Morocco in her plane. So, on one of her trips to Tangiers with two clients (and myself) we had the opportunity to fly over The Rock and have a bird's eye view. On landing, we all inspected the plot of land. More interestingly for me, we had lunch at the Moroccan restaurant, nine courses of tapas salad just for five Euros each (including a plate of chips as well!). We were home late in the afternoon. I can still taste the pickled turnips, fried aubergine with eggs, sweet chillies, potato with yoghurt, grilled fish, delicious chick peas, green peppers, cucumber, sweet tomatoes, radishes and lettuce with Moroccan pita bread - all washed down with fresh mint tea. The place has changed completely since I came over with Jan about ten years ago, when we could not get out of our hotel without getting hassled by a carpet seller or young people who want to improve their English by tricking you into going to their uncle's jewellery shop. It was so bad back then that many older visitors did not come out of their hotels for fear of being hassled. On this trip, nobody bothered us as I had been told that a new young king made a law so that visitors cannot be approached unless they approached you first. Mind you, we also had a local minder to protect us.

I got a strange feeling about Gibraltar. The place is of strategic importance to England as it is the gateway to the Mediterranean and, with ships coming from the black sea and through the Suez canal, everyone has to pass through this Strait. So, rather we keep it in our control than anybody else's! Of course it is a busy place for smugglers, dodgy wheeling and dealing in high finance and get-rich-quick schemes. I must say there are numerous (and perfectly legal) businesses offering offshore tax-free deals. You only have to look at the many brass plates of various companies on each door you pass. There must be a link with the sneaky monkey of Gibraltar and business! I sat on a cemetery park bench watching the world go by, and I wondered whether that man was walking hurriedly to keep his rendezvous with some immigrant smuggler, wondered who the pretty young lady was, maybe a dealer in white gold? I don't know, I got carried away in my wild dreams due the mysterious reputation of The Rock. I was there only few hours and left with such a strange feeling.

Do you know where The Rock got its name? It was given by Moorish bourbon that they were trying to get into Spain and finally they succeeded in gaining a foothold at Tarifa, only a stone's throw away from Gibraltar. The whole coastal area from Cadiz to Tarifa is exciting except the port of Algeciras. It is a shitty place, full of high concrete blocks, seedy and ugly to the extreme. You get the feeling of dens full of dubious characters. The port pollutes the atmosphere and environment with its industrial smoke and you see hundreds of Moroccans discharging from the ferry at the terminal, wearing colourful djelabas and carrying unbelievable loads of luggage like snails carry their homes on their backs. I did not even stop for coffee and headed towards Tarifa thirsty and hungry.

I was rewarded immediately with the fantastic view of the Strait as I went up the road with the magnificent rolling hill and strong wind. I came across sign for a hotel restaurant and wondering what to do when my eye caught the roadblock by the traffic police half a mile ahead. That made my mind for me, I simply made the U-turn and headed for the Hotel restaurant. What a find. It was the best stop of the day, warm log fire in the reception hall with smiling senoritas to attend to you. A big dining room filled with travellers having their lunch and the aromas of good cooking were evident in abundance and made your mouth water. I checked in and the receptionist took me to my room, we passed palm trees and various decorations in the style and fashion of the 1930s. It must be a favourite place for the American exploring Africa, landing at Gibraltar or at Algeciras and resting in this magnificent posh hotel or simply stopping for good spot of lunch. The place had a feel of class, it had a swimming pool and outdoor shade for summer visitors. My room overlooked the strait, a stream flowed through the natural park of the hotel with water cascading down the hill. It even had a miniature bullring, mercifully no longer in use. My bathroom was bigger than the bedroom. I thought this was valuable information - if you're passing by, there's no need to book twin rooms if you're travelling with lots of kids! I had a pleasant and delicious lunch with really nice Rioja, and spent the afternoon exploring the hotel's park, growing purple violets, cork and the odd mimosa tree laden with bright yellow buds.

Late afternoon I buzzed off to Tarifa, only about ten kilometres away. To my surprise I heard great squeals and thunder noises, there was lots of wind and you really had to hold your steering wheel firmly otherwise you were a goner. Twists and turns nearly changed my mind. I almost decided not to go to Tarifa and to go back to the comfort of the hotel instead. Pondering this dilemma I reached the summit and saw hundreds of windmills propelling away, all producing electricity for the Spanish grid. I never saw so many wind turbines at one place in one batch. I found a parking spot and came out of the car, letting the thunder of the turbines cause me fear and excitement. You have to be very brave to go near the windmill and take a photograph just in case the wind lifts you up and you are history. I was breathless with hill walking and fear, and took the greatest care getting back into the car, turned around and headed back onto the road to Tarifa.

Tarifa is known in the geography books as the last town on the European continent before Africa starts, only 30 minutes away by hydrofoil. Moors had many battles there to conquer Spain and legend has it that once the castle was under siege in 1492 and the local infamous commander Guzman's nine year old son was taken hostage by the Spanish traitors. The Moors demanded the surrender of the garrison in exchange for the boy's life, but Commander Guzman's loyalty to his country got the better of him and he offered his own dagger to do the dirty deed. Do not let this tragic story put you off visiting the town, though! Tarifa is very Moorish, a labyrinth of narrow streets leading up to great open courtyards full of restaurants and coffee bars. It has the atmosphere of North Africa. Golden sandy beaches miles and miles long and prolonged spells of strong wind coming from the Strait are ideal for water sports, water gliding, windsurfing, and water kites in those miles of empty space with abundant caravan parks.

I liked the area, so I stayed for two days and then headed for Cadiz to see where the Armada set sail to England to meet its fate at the hands of Sir Walter Raleigh and the English weather. Nelson had his victory at Trafalgar, attacking Spanish and French ships coming out to sea from the shelter of Cadiz harbour so I wanted to visit this historic town and feel the atmosphere of a bygone age. It is a truly magical place that you need another visit to get to know the real feel of the history and culture of the city.

So when Jan came over from England on her Easter break we headed for that famous highway hotel and restaurant on the N340 to Tarifa. We visited Jerez for a day to see its world famous sherry distilleries and Moorish castle, a rare treat for the English, and finally landed in Cadiz. This was the real thrill of our tour. Our hotel was in the old town, and we went round and round in our brand new Yaris but could not find the hotel. In the end Jan got out of the car and walked about, finding the hotel in a narrow street with no access to cars. Where's the bloody car park as we have reserved our car parking with the hotel accommodation! We were told that we have to go back a few miles then return by another street that we would find, at the back of the hotel, a NO ENTRY street. The receptionist told us to take no notice of the sign. 'Just go in and there will be a man standing there from the hotel and he will let you in.'

'Let us in where? We do not see any car park and street is not wide enough to swing the cat never mind our new

Yaris!' They insisted that we follow the instructions on the map. So we did.

I tell you, the traffic in Cadiz is dreadful, you need a bottle of brandy with you to calm the nerves, and all these delivery vans and cars just drove me round the bend! Anyhow, we carried on as English people do. Mind you, Jan was looking in the back seat for that bottle of sherry we bought for our friends in England to crack open and be done with it. We arrived after a near miss with the local bus. The hotel porter was suddenly standing in the middle of the street and was waving his hands frantically, so we took Dutch courage and slowly advanced toward the porter without scratching the car, Jan was having kittens. There, at an angle of 45°, there was a little space for the car to go in and face a locked aluminium door. The porter pressed a button, and after five minutes the door wandered upward in an unhurried motion to reveal a lift.

Our jaws dropped and the car went forward, then the door slid away and a giant car park appeared three storeys underground. Miracles do happen! We headed straight for the swimming pool and Turkish bath. We dared not to ask for directions as we could only see the big and beautiful courtyard of the hotel and tower block of bedrooms. We followed the signs of pool to a series of rooms and a lift. We went a further four storeys down and there we saw a magic swimming pool glittering in deep blue sea colour brim with floating lemons and oranges in the pool inviting us to dive in and all was forgiven. The next two days were spent strolling narrow Moorish alleyways and having delicious Cadiz cuisine and coffee.

-22-
Hooked

After Gibraltar I needed some calm in my life, so I decided to spend more time daydreaming on the beach. I was there in less than fifteen minutes after I decided I was going. The sea had those calm waves that fishermen die for.

I put my beach mat out, put my umbrella up, sat in my chair and cast off.

'Yeeoow!' I felt a sharp pain in my right ear as the fishing hook ripped through it, almost removing it completely. I started to panic. I wished desperately that Jan were there. First she would have told me off, and then she would have helped me. I wouldn't have minded her grumbling if it meant that I would get a kiss on my ear to make it better. Then I could have laid down on the mat and rested my head on her sweet-smelling, cuddly body and gone to heaven.

But it was no good. I had to get a hold of my own panic. I loosened the line and released the hook from my ear without getting my fingers hooked in the process – a very delicate operation indeed. Then I realised that blood was pouring down the side of my neck. I was beginning to understand how fish feel when they get caught on the hook. I knew that was the end of fishing for that day – and maybe forever.

I was exhausted and my ear would not stop bleeding, partly because of my diabetes and also because I take two aspirin a day to thin my blood for the sake of my angina.

I was starting to look like someone who had cut his own throat. The blood was now running down my chest. I unwrapped my sandwiches and pressed the tissue they were wrapped in against my ear. Then I pressed a slice of bread there too. I'd lost the chicken, tomato and chicory, but something had to be sacrificed and the seagulls were pleased.

I made my way home, determined not to fish for a long time.

-23-
Romeria Festival

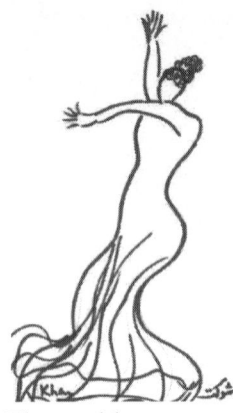

In May, in Almayate, there is a Christian festival called Romeria. Everyone gets dressed up in multi-coloured flamenco style clothes, each outfit beautifully handmade and finished with matching dancing shoes and a Spanish hair-do with lots of flowers. The festival celebrates the culture of Gypsies, as there were many in Almayate.

The residents get on their horses and proceed 10km to Velez, a province of Malaga, where there is a large Gypsy population. Alongside the couples riding horses, people danced and sang in the street. If they didn't have a horse, they drove their bullock carts, which were decorated in flowers and banners.

The procession left Almayate church at 9am and about halfway through the trip they reached Torre del Mar. Lunch was served in various restaurants before the journey was completed at Velez. There was more singing, dancing and drinking there, then the procession reversed. By the time it reached Torre del Mar on the way back, people were so drunk they were falling off their horses like apples from trees, causing great thumps that caused the horses to bolt. Also by this time, the bulls that were pulling various carts were started to look slightly aggressive.

Back at Almayate church, the statue of Christ was put away safely and everyone moved to the bodega to watch a video tape of the day and drink more Rioja.

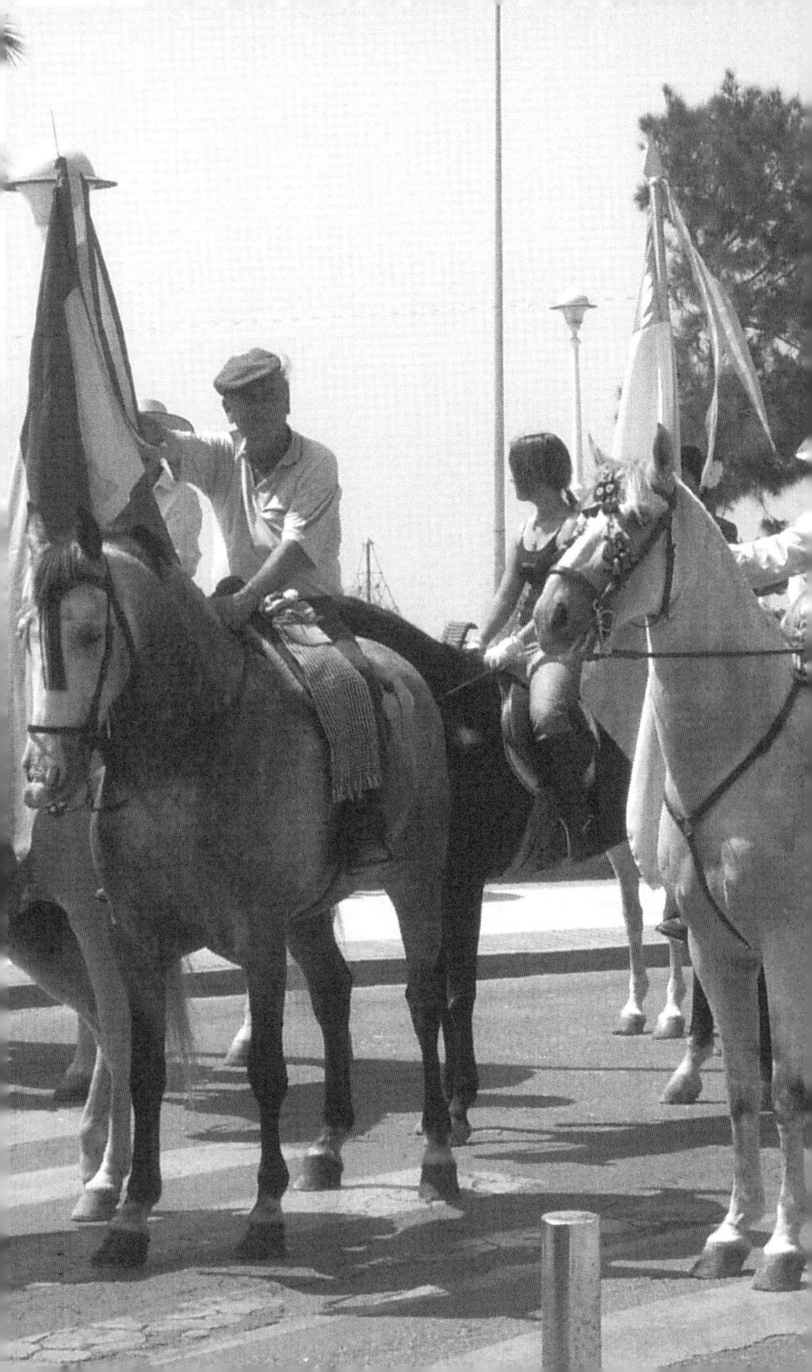

-24-
Creepy-Crawly

Spain is full of exotic animals and insects. But wherever you find insects and rodents, you have snakes to keep the balance of nature.

I am a lover of nature and have devoted my whole life to studying it. I have spent more time watching David Attenborough on TV than I ever did listening to lectures on botany and zoology at university.

After watching Sir David's programmes, I know there's a lake in Africa where flies gather in such numbers that day turns to night and the lake falls under darkness. Local fishermen catch these flies to supplement the protein deficiencies in their diet.

I know there are sea turtles hundreds of years old that weigh one hundred pounds. They struggle a few hundred yards up the beach, dig a metre-deep hole with their flippers, lay hundreds of eggs, and then bury them – and that is the end of their parental duties. When the cute baby turtles hatch, they make a life or death dash for the ocean – and the cycle of life goes on for another generation.

I know a giraffe's birth is miraculous. The baby survives a great fall from its mother's womb. It struggles to its feet, such an easy target for hyenas and lions.

All the beauty in nature thrills me. David Attenborough's programmes thrill me. But there's one animal that sends shivers down my spine.

The snake.

It is their creeping, wriggling nature. You do not know where they are going, and they have gone in a split second. You see them, and then you don't see them. They slip away as quickly as they come.

India is full of snakes. The city is alive with them, snake charmers on every corner with their cobras. The countryside teems with snakes. You see them in the paddy fields and on the dirt tracks. You come across a snake and a giant, squirrel-like mongoose fighting to the death; a good show for the village children.

But I never got used to the snakes. When I was a student, I caught a snake in the dried canal bed. The snake was about a metre long, as fat as a sugar cane stick. I killed it, and bottled it and filled the bottle with formaldehyde and kept it in my room for days. I stuffed it and gave to the college's science faculty.

But I still have a snake phobia.

A snake slid into my home in Lahore. It was about a half a metre long and slithered from underneath a wooden plank in the corner of the courtyard, flicking his long tongue. Commotion erupted when we all saw this wriggling thing on the cobblestones. Dogs, cats, birds – and my brother, sister, mother and father – tried to avoid the creature.

I climbed on the Charpi (bedstead) as my father rushed around to find a stick with which to beat the snake. My brothers, sister and mother cried and screamed. The dog barked and tired to bite the invader. Then the snake found a hole in the courtyard wall and disappeared. For days nobody went near that hole. My father plugged it with cement. But I'm sure the snake got away – perhaps next door to scare our neighbours.

Almayate was full of snakes. It is a rural hillside village near the sea with rodents and insects – an ideal breeding ground for snakes.

When you are out for a hillside walk you can see them curled up, basking in the sun. You have to be careful when picking wild almonds, fruits and flowers. You can easily pick up a little stick – until it develops a life of its own; and you can accidentally tread on them if you are walking in long grass — a nasty surprise!

The children in Almayate are not frightened of snakes. They keep them in their pockets and play with them. When an old house was demolished to make way for several modern houses near my villa, they found a snake den. The snakes slithered out of there in their hundreds – all sizes, wriggling away in all directions, and residents were busy clearing them out of their houses for weeks.

I did not know the story of the snake den when I moved in. I admired the empty space in front of my villa where the old house had once stood because it gave me more space to park my car.

The morning after the Romeria, I went shopping. When I came home, I put what I'd bought on the table and out of the corner of my eye saw a flick of something whipping across the marble floor. I had no idea what it was – just a flash of a black and white, about 30cm long.

I turned to look and to my horror I saw this nasty, wriggly thing curled on the floor. I panicked and ran out to the courtyard. I was out of breath. I did not know what to do. I had no idea what the Spanish word for snake was. I called my neighbour but couldn't explain. So I crept back into the house, watching for that snake.

I went upstairs trying to find my Spanish dictionary. I found it in the bedroom. Looking for a, b, c ... ah 's', 's for snake'. Serpentine. I got hold of a fly swatter and went downstairs. I was shaking. I had the dictionary in one hand and fly killer in the other. I sneaked up on the snake and – bang, bang, bang over its head.

I felt very uncomfortable in the house. I used to enter in a rather comical way; like Peter Sellers in the Pink Panther movies trying to catch a thief. I always looked at the floor in case I trod on another creepy-crawly snake.

Three weeks after the snake incident, Jan arrived from England. She saw my funny walk and asked what was the matter with me. I dare not tell her the full story because she is more afraid of snakes than I am – and she never watches nature programmes on TV in case there are snakes in them. I bribed all my neighbours and told them not to mention the snake episode. In fact, I begged them not to bring the subject up at all with my wife. She would have fainted at the merest mention of snakes.

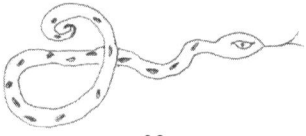

-25-
Water Crisis

May Day was hot.

I usually needed my morning shower to get me going, and it set me up for the whole day. I should've watered the garden the night before, but I was lazy; I left that for May Day morning.

I was woken up by the dawn. I went downstairs, made tea with some bottled water, and took it up to the balcony. I watched the fishermen bringing in their night catch. The nets were loaded to the brim. The boats struggled to sail into harbour under the weight.

My next-door neighbour's canaries chirped and I thought about what a wonderful morning it was.

I had my morning cuppa and drew some sketches for the day's painting. Then I went to the bathroom and stripped off, ready for my morning shower. I turned on the water, and waited to be refreshed. I waited. And waited. And then I waited. No water. Oh, Hell! Had we been cut off?

I did get a lot of reminders about an unpaid water bill in the name of the previous owner. I had written to the water board several times, giving them my bank details and telling them I was the owner, and asking for a new bill. But they'd cut me off.

What was I going to do? It was Friday and the weekend was already ruined.

I got dressed and went downstairs to check the meter. There was no sign that the water had been cut off, and I thought I needed a plumber. Maybe there was a problem with the water storage tank, I thought. I climbed into the loft and checked the tank. No problem there, either.

I needed a plumber, and I had no idea how to ask for one in Spanish.

I found my dictionary and discovered that 'plumber' is 'fontanero'. I phoned an old friend, hoping she would ask her landlord if he knew a 'fontanero'.

I had to get a plumber. Without water the garden would be ruined by the end of the evening. The plants were already wilting. But that was my fault, because I should have watered them the previous evening, as I usually did. I cursed myself for being lazy.

Six months of hard labour would bear no fruit if I couldn't get water soon. And with all the panic and the stress, I'd started to sweat – which, because I'd not had a shower, made me stink even more.

I wondered if my neighbours could help. They would have water. I could bring over some water in cans, have a wash and also water the plants a little.

I rush next door and looked for Anna Senior.

I said, 'Anna, Anna, no aqua – casa. No aqua casa.'

She wasn't there. I went to her neighbours' house. Crowds of women were gathered in the courtyard. They were distributing strawberries. Someone handed me a tray full of fruit.

I told Anna Senior that I had no water in the house, and asked her if she could give me some water. I said all this in broken Spanish, and everyone looked at me with surprise.

Someone said, 'Did you not know that the water has been cut off at the mains for the whole village and it will be cut off for three days?'

What was I going to do?

Luckily, Anna Senior had some already stored in watering cans, which, of course, she very kindly shared with me.

-26-
My Depression

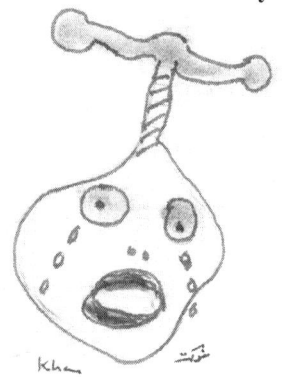

Black clouds gathered in Almayate. I had a telephone call from Lahore. My mother was in a coma and the doctors weren't hopeful. But she'd had a wonderful life. She was well over 80.

My sister said that mother had been calling my name: 'Shaukat, Shaukat.' My sister told her that she would fetch me so she went outside and came back wrapped up in men's clothes and pretended to be me.

I thought of all the good times I had with my mother. Once my father lost his temper and tried to beat me up. She locked me in a room and stood outside to protect me.

I remember her tears when I was in Mayo hospital, Lahore, with a badly infected appendix. She sat up all night, holding my hand until my temperature dropped to normal. I felt her soft, sensitive hands brushing my face from time to time, and I heard her whispered prayers for my recovery.

When she came to England she spent all her time at Canterbury's Marks and Spencer. Filling her trolley with food, she could not get over the freshness, quality and variety – and best of all you could pick from the shelves yourself and take it away.

In Lahore, there were no supermarkets at all at that time and trading was still done in the old-fashioned bazaar style. It was pot-luck when it came to quality and freshness.

I also showed off by taking her to my bank's hole-in-the-wall. I entered my pin number and told her to press the cash button, and out came the money. She thought that's how we got our money in England – not by working, but simply by tapping numbers out in a machine in the wall.

My mother is the last member of my family who does not understand why the English left India.

Kind Boat Lady – the Adventures of a Nightingale

When I settled in Almayate, I started to meet British residents at the bars and cafés.

One name kept creeping into the conversation; the Kind Boat Lady who lived in Calata Marina on her vessel. She took people on trips out to sea for 20 euros. This included a tapas lunch and drinks.

The Kind Boat Lady – KBL – has a generous nature. If she found a dead fish on the water, she would take it to the vet and get him to try and revive it. Her boat was called Sea Goddess. It was a wonderful little boat, ideal for short trips to go and watch dolphins, do a bit of fishing, and if you were brave, dive in and have a swim. I always find swimming in the sea exhilarating and refreshing. It is one of the holiday experiences you should not miss.

KBL's life was full of exciting and adventurous stories. She was a dietician and worked in a hospital in the North in England, where she found a lot of undernourished Indian and Pakistani patients in her ward. To find out more about their diet and culture, she decided to go to India.

She wrote to various hospitals in India and went to Bombay, Calcutta, Delhi, Jaipur, Masour, Lakhnow and Hyderabad.

She arrived in a YMCA hostel in Bombay and after checking in she opened her backpack to put her clothes away. She was looking forward to a refreshing shower. But rats had chewed her clothes and the water had been cut off for the day – hey, I know the feeling.

On her first day in the YMCA, she had holes in her clothes and no water to wash with.

But however grim her first days were, she had a wonderful time in India. She learned a great deal about people's eating habits and their culture. She stayed for two years.

Then she travelled to Dubai, and worked in a hospital there. She met Pakistanis, Indians, Arabs, and Europeans. She discovered that different people got different pay for the same work. Americans were the highest paid, then the Europeans, the Arabs next, and second from the bottom of the pay scale were the Indians, Pakistanis and Filipinos. Sri Lankans and Bangladeshis came last.

KBL applied for a job in Guyana in South America. The reply said, 'If you wish to come to this hell-hole of a hospital full of rats, flies, flooded floors due to a leaking roof, shortages of medicines and apparatus, and do lots of hard work for very low pay, you are most welcome.'

She could not resist the challenge and gave up the comfort and luxury of Dubai Hospital, and went to Guyana.

KBL discovered that the locally nutritious foods such as bananas and peanuts were neglected in favour of imported foods. She devised recipes from locally grown produce and organised a street fair to popularise it. The locals realised immediately how good it was for them. The fair was a great success. Unfortunately, she told a reporter about her nutrition plan, and the paper ran a story, which said a European woman was encouraging locals to eat their own, healthy, foods instead of the imported stuff. Her superior reprimanded her.

The success of KBL's fair got her invited to the Los Angeles Nutrition Conference – but unfortunately she was not allowed to go. A Guyanan was sent to represent Guyana's interests instead.

KBL kept improving the food, though. She discovered that local prison staff baked bread for the hospital where she worked. The prison was a few miles away. The bread was baked and put into sacks, then brought to the hospital by prisoners. By the time it arrived in the hospital, it was hard like a football.

KBL had some wooden boxes designed with small compartments to hold the freshly cooked bread. For a while, at least, the patients had soft, tasty fresh bread for their dinner. But this only lasted a few weeks. The prisoners chopped the heavy boxes into firewood.

Hospital patients were served food cold because the kitchens were far away from the wards. Negotiating lots of stairs to bring the food to the patient was difficult. The food was carried on the nurses' heads.

When KBL was in England on holiday, she found a company that had insulated food boxes. She asked them to donate the boxes to her hospital so the patients could have hot food. The company agreed and containers were donated to the hospital. They were accepted, with pomp and ceremony, by a government minister.

Unfortunately the insulated food containers ended up in army camps and the patients never got hot food.

This was the last straw for KBL, so she left Guyana, but feels it was fun and worthwhile and a satisfactory cause because every day was full of excitement and adventure.

She met exciting people on her boat trips and they became good friends. One couple she met in the bar didn't have much money left for their honeymoon, and they needed cheap accommodation. She offered them her two-bedroom Pablo free for their honeymoon.

Pablo means a little Spanish house. KBL bought it for only three thousand euros and spent another three thousand to put in a loo, shower and an extra room. For the total cost of six thousand euros she got this beautiful two-bedroom Pablo, which she keeps for needy friends who want cheap holiday accommodation – or anyone stranded and fallen on hard times. This is the nature and character of KBL.

-28-
Dehydration

It was the end of May and the last week had been difficult. I had almost run out of my allowance of money and had to be frugal. I budgeted for a certain amount each month and was always strict with myself, not borrowing from the month ahead.

I had to be a miser, saving money on bottles of water or sun tan lotion, buying cheap fruit and vegetables and cheap chicken pieces. I couldn't go to restaurants. I had to read old newspapers. I couldn't take the car anywhere to save on fuel.

I was making myself thoroughly sick and tired, and I felt stupid.

But the beginning of the month meant I could fill the car with diesel. I could go to a restaurant. I could buy an English newspaper.

So June 1, the beginning of the month, was good news for me as I could allow myself to go to the cashpoint, put my plastic in and punch in my pin number – if I still remembered it. Sometimes I forgot it and had to come home and try to remember where I filed it. Sometimes it took all day and involved a complete search of my filing 'system'.

The files got scattered on the bed. They got re-checked, re-checked, and re-checked. Still no pin number. I phoned Jan in England to see if she remembered where I'd scribbled down the bloody number.

In the end, you are exhausted and your brain does not function.

I'd have a cup of tea, and get out an old newspaper. I had piles and piles of them. I did not have the heart to throw them away for the whole year. They cost three times as much in Spain as they do in Britain, so it wasn't that easy to chuck them out with the rubbish.

I'd read Cherie Blair's flat saga over a hundred times and knew the story inside out.

After reading this nonsense again, I put my jacket on and went for a walk to calm down. I put my hand in the top pocket to get my magnifying glass out. I carried it to observe wild flowers. I found a little notebook in the pocket, the one in which I noted my flower observations.

Looking at it I see that it was also where I wrote down my pin number. It was there on the cover. The bloody pin number. It was logical wasn't it? If I'd lost this flower notebook, who would have known what these numbers were for? Flower drawings and names like ovary, stamen, stigma, florets, stamens, bract, sepals and petals; descriptions and notes about enlarged ovaries would have fooled them. They would think it is the work of a sex maniac and throw it away. My pin number would have been safe from fraud.

I strolled down to the cash dispenser and got some money, before heading home. I drove to Torre del Mar, only a five minute drive, and bought the Sunday Times. Parking the car, I placed the disabled permit on the dashboard. It was a habit. In Spain they only had very few spaces for disabled parking in the whole town – and they were near a rubbish bin.

My car was full of dents. One was from Nerja, and one was from Malaga, one from Victoria - quite a collection!

I strolled down to the cyber café and checked my email, and after that I walked on the promenade. I sat on the bench and read the Sunday Times. I wished I didn't buy the papers - the Blairs again, although now it was Mr Blair.

After reading the paper, I went to the beach by car, which is another five minutes drive. I always had a folding chair, umbrella, fishing gear, sketch book and reading books, towel and beach mat in the boot. I spent the whole day fishing, reading, sketching – all I had was a hamburger and beer from the beach café.

I got home at about 6pm feeling very tired. I had an evening meal, watched TV. I went to bed with a headache and could not get to sleep. My head was going round and round with strange logic. I had a night of this. But that's what you get for being silly, and not drinking enough water. I spent all day on the beach without liquid in my body, dehydrating myself – I was going to have some very silly dreams.

-29-
Kitty Love

One night I was awoken by a commotion. There was screaming, running about, and scuffling.

I thought I was dreaming, but a little later on, I heard the same racket again, both close by and in the distance.

In the morning, I had nothing but a faint memory of this disturbance. I got up, made a cup of tea, opened the shutters to let the sun and air into the house and went out onto the patio garden.

A nasty, sticky, foul smell hung in the air. It reminded me of the smell you sometimes find under trees, when walking in the park. Of course, when I thought of the park, I thought of dogs and the unpleasant smells they leave behind. But I knew this couldn't be the problem. How the hell could a dog get into my gated courtyard?

The only dog near here is my neighbour's dog, Chippie. And he is on the other side of the street behind a wall he cannot jump. Chippie is a small, mongrel-like terrier dog and unless he could locate and use a Spanish street map and a trampoline, I did not think it could be him.

Mind you, he is a very obedient and clever dog. When his owner calls him, 'Chippie, oh Chippie', he curls around her legs and hides his head under her skirt.

She is very proud of this 'love and affection trick'. But Chippie does not like foreigners.

I park my car near to his wall sometimes and one day, I forgot he was there and looked over the wall, right at him. Suddenly Chippie jumped in the air and nearly got my ear.

I was taken aback, lost my balance and fell on my parked car. Of course, I understand that Chippie was defending his territory but sometimes, I go out onto my balcony and make faces at him. He just rises above such childish behaviour and ignores me, which annoys me even more.

If I try to be friendly with him and say 'Buenos Dias', in the morning, he just barks and barks in a nasty way. I don't think we are ever going to be friends. Even his owner has tried, but Chippie just curls his face in her skirt and wiggles his tail, as if to say, 'I do not want to be friendly to this bloody foreigner from England. He makes faces at me from his balcony'.

So, the smell in the garden cannot be the smell of a dog.

Then it clicked. We have neighbours on my right and the neighbour has got cats, and cats can climb the garden wall and, for all I know, may be able to unlock the gate. I am sure they come to my garden when I am asleep and sit on my chairs and hold conferences, discussing villagers, hunting territories, and other feline issues.

A few days ago I saw a couple of tomcats meowing in an aggressive way. It went on for a long time and became rather a nuisance. I noticed they were making territory markings with their pee all over the place. This was obviously the smell. My garden was full of my neighbour's cats.

One cat was on heat and the Toms were after her, trying to mate. I have never seen cats mating, but I'm a curious sort of person, so as soon as I heard them, making their aggressive meows, I went to the balcony with my binoculars - there was no time to pull faces at Chippie that day.

The Tom went up to the lady cat, jumped on her, trying to hold her neck in his mouth and lay down on top of her body. She growled and protested and kept her tail firmly down over her back-end. The Tom made more aggressive noises and forced himself on her, but she would not have it.

Then another Tom came by and tried to muscle in. By this point it was getting rather noisy. All of a sudden, due to infighting between the two Toms for prime position, the female cat squirmed free and was off.

The chase was on then, over the rooftops, the gardens, the streets, courtyards, away the three of them went, flying and hissing and marking their territory, peeing as they went, all over my flowers.

The last I saw there were three toms chasing this poor cat, which at some point, must have given in.

Surely, it cannot be love.

-30-
My Garden

I loved my little patio garden. This is what I lived for. Early in the morning, when I opened my front door, there it was – welcoming me with its scent and its colours: purple, pale cream, yellow, lipstick red and pink, whites and blues, all the flowers standing upright and beaming.

There was jasmine in white blossom intertwined with bougainvillea of all colours. The scent of lemon, tangerine and grapefruit blossom sharpened up your senses. The most expensive perfume is made from the essential oil of orange flowers, which is called neroli.

The floor of the patio was covered with asparagus ferns, busy lizzie and geraniums, which were dotted around in little pots. I also had four different varieties of palm trees. Near the palm trees I had plumago, which has sky blue clusters of flowers, creeping around the palm tree.

Next to the palm tree there was a magic plant from the east: frangipani. It is the plant of the Gods. The Hindus plant it in temples and its flowers are used to make frangipani perfume.

Two bay trees, each about one metre high, stood outside the door. Alongside stood a pomegranate tree and rat-ki-rani. This plant is famous in India where it is called Queen of the Night. In the evening its clusters of small flowers open and the scent drives you crazy. In Spain it is also known as Dama de Noche.

My little patio garden was 20ft wide and 14ft deep, with wrought iron gates and a terrace wall that was one and half metres tall all around it. It had 30 large plants in pots and two beds containing bougainvilleas, cannas lilies, arum lilies, hibiscus, geranium, busy-lizzies and scented syringa (mock orange).

I also had a small pot of mint and lemon verbena, which made delicious tea. I watered my garden every night, at about eleven o'clock in the summer, and three times a week in winter. Once a month I fed the plants with liquid fertiliser and once a week I would go around with secateurs to get rid of deadwood and unwanted flowers.

Lots of local butterflies and small birds visited my garden. When my next-door neighbours came at the weekend, they put their canary cages near my garden when the birds sang. It was like listening to Mozart and The Beatles at the same time.

When I was away my neighbour looked after, and watered, my garden. She seemed to water too much, and often when I returned there were one or two casualties because of over-watering. But it was a small price to pay to save the rest.

I had a small table and three chairs where I sat and thought of all the gardens I had visited in the world, and how I could squeeze in another plant pot here and there. I had to control my emotions when I visited any garden centre, or I'd bankrupt myself buying everything in sight.

I sometimes had my morning cup of tea and breakfast in my patio garden. And on summer evenings I would sit there listening to classical music, the Mediterranean breeze brushing my face. It was the best relaxation and pleasure you could experience; a glass of tinto in my little garden.

-31-
It's Our Pleasure

When I found my dream villa, I brought Jan to Spain to sign the contract. The *escritura* is the proof of purchase, if you have not got this document for the property you are buying than you have no legal proof of ownership. Watch out and ensure that when you purchase the property it has an escritura. This document gives the details of the ownership of the house, declaration of the property tax paid and legal authority of building status, to ensure it is not built illegally. It is essentially the Spanish form of a property deed.

We stayed in a small hotel near Calata harbour. This hotel did not have a restaurant, but opposite the hotel just across the A340 main road there are three or four restaurants, which provide excellent breakfast, lunch and evening meals. We found one particular restaurant in a cul-de-sac, hemmed in between blocks of flats. Typical local fishermen's dens, packed with lot of local characters and full of Spanish atmosphere. It is called La Fuentes Casa Manolo. Roughly translated: The House of the Fountain of Mr Manolo. It has traditional local dishes such as spiced octopus with fresh tomato sauce and loads of garlic. Swordfish steak grill with olive oil and of course, for holidaymakers, egg, chips and ham, and a good stock of Rioja. We had many meals at this restaurant, whenever Jan came to spend her holidays with me at Almayate. It's only few kilometers from the villa, going north towards Narja, just a five minute drive away.

I always spend May in England, as England is at its best in the season of spring, everything is sparkling new and fresh. Orchids in full blossom, hedgerows bursting with wild flowers of pink, mauve and white. Village greens in ship-shape, people busy spring cleaning. Flower shows and garden fêtes in full swing all over the country. Nothing better to do than stroll around to the local village hall, have homemade scones with jam and tea, visit the flower show, come home with bag full of fresh vegetables and bunch of flowers, a jar of four fruit marmalade and jelly and apple pie. Weather turns a little warmer and people shed their winter clothes. Everybody more or less in a happy mood, looking forward to summer. Foreign birds migrating in for the summer riches of England in the marshes, meadows and countryside, all in all there is a buzz of life. I like all this activity, of course, and in the county of Kent, the famous Garden of England, blossoms are everywhere in the countryside. The AA, the Automobile Association, put signs in the county for the benefit of their members' blossom tour. Artists are out capturing landscape of bluebells in the woods. Muster fields, a riot of gold yellow colour, the green shoots of hops, trailing, twining and twisting on the pole, birds gathering nesting material and fox cubs coming out of their dens to play. It's a month of magic and excitement. I would not miss May in England for all the tea in china.

Jan built up some extra ten days of holidays by working overtime in the winter, she decided to have her ten days in Almayate to relax in the pool near the villa, on the beach. She also took advantage of a five pound air ticket from Manston airport to Malaga. This was a new cheap fare airline from Kent promoting their new routes to Malaga and other destination in Europe. This is a blessing for us. No more lengthy, complicated, awful rail travel to

Gatwick, goodbye to Tunbridge and Redhill stations, goodbye to miles of walking in the Gatwick terminal to board the plane. No nightmare of getting up middle of the night, worrying about missing the plane due to delays on the train or anywhere else. Manston airport is only ten miles from Canterbury, it takes just twenty minutes to get to the airport and you park your car for just five pounds a day, a bargain! Walk a few yards and you are in the terminal, checking in, through the security and on the plane, which is parked just outside the door. The whole job takes half an hour, what a treat, hope they stay in business and God bless all those who fly with EUJet at Manston, Kent.

In the first week of June we arrived at Almayate. We'd caught the 9:40 plane in the morning at Manston. It'd been quite a drama. Nerves were shattered. I was taken ill suddenly, landed up in casualty at the Canterbury hospital, so Jan decided to cancel her holidays, she also rang to EUJet to cancel the flight, but they said it couldn't be cancelled but it could be changed to another flight date. This meant we would have to pay extra airport taxes which were not worth it. By the way, they did not have a record for Mr. Khan's booking either - some mix up in the computer system.

I was kept in for one night for observation at the hospital then discharged as a false alarm. Sigh of relief. Apologised to the consultant for wasting his and the hospital's time but he assured me, graveyards are full of dead bodies where people have not bothered to go to hospital because it may be just a chest pain and paid the price dearly by having a heart attack instead. It is better to be safe than sorry as I've already had a triple bypass, nine angioplasties and spinal stonosis, stomach ulcers, kidney problems and, not to be missed, diabetes. I had better take care of myself. Anyhow, after a dreadful night at the hospital keeping all the patients in the ward up all night by my snoring I was to be discharged in the morning. Must have been a blessing for everyone. After the good news, I came home and suggested to Jan we should go to Spain if her office agreed to un-cancel her holidays and the airline managed to sort out my ticket.

Luckily Jan got her holiday reinstated and also sorted out my ticket. We were all set for Spain. Jan was worried that her office desk was not being left in good order, as she left her office in a panic due to my sudden hospital admission. It was decided we had to leave early in the morning for Whitstable to get to her office. We made her office desk tidy and left urgent matters and instructions to her colleague. It was all done in a matter of twenty minutes while I waited at the Sainsbury's supermarket nearby polishing off an English breakfast - egg, beans, mushroom, tomatoes and sausages with tea and bread and butter. We were at the airport in just ten minutes, with half an hour to spare for the flight. I bought bundles of various English newspapers for my reading in Spain, and a drum of Pringles for munching on the plane. They are a kind of crisp and so bloody good that you have to finish the whole drum in one go. We arrived at Almayate by the late afternoon in high spirits and looking forward to a relaxing holiday. Barbequed sardines for lunch by the swimming pool, washed down with a glass of rioja and plenty of sunshine, forgetting all the worry of unstable angina and the grey clouds of England. We had a comfortable night at the villa after getting plastered with local tinto at the La Papemolina, the famous local bogeda. Next morning I was straight off to the beachside pool reading John Sergeant's book.

What an enjoyable life that sod is having. He seems to be at the right place at the right time, all the time. I wished that Margaret Thatcher had handbagged him good and proper in Paris so he had something to moan about! He seems to have had a lot of friends to do him favours all the time. How many lives cats have! He must have had more than nine so far. Well, I wish him well. You have to admit he is like a chocolate bar, very tasty indeed.

In the evening, we decided to pay a visit to our favourite restaurant at Caleta. The restaurant is called La Fuente, and we had a delicious dinner. Jan had a house salad for starter, and for the main course, grilled swordfish. I had a fish soup with all the shellfish of Spain in it and the spicy octopus with fresh, homemade tomato sauce and potatoes, and of course another bottle of the very best Rioja. After doing 'ooh!', 'ahh!' and 'yum yum yum!', I paid the bill and walked off to the Caleta marina for coffee. We'd had an enjoyable evening and drove back home at what must have been about midnight. Went straight to bed, too stuffed and drunk to have any hanky-panky. In the morning after a breakfast of melon, peaches, fresh orange juice, croissant with marmalade and English pot of tea, I packed up the bag for the beach and was almost ready to go. 'Hang on, hang on!' I said to Jan, who was already shouting to go.

'What about some money for the lunch?'

'Where is my bloody wallet?' It *was* in my pocket. I searched all my pockets inside out again and again. Then Jan ran in from the courtyard, where she'd been waiting to go.

'Let me have a look!'

'Don't you trust me?'

'Frankly, no.' She proceeded to look in my pockets.

'Not that bit!' I said, 'Just concentrate on the wallet.'

'No, it doesn't seem to be there,' she said in a disappointed manner. No luck then. 'You must have put it in the bedside drawers before you retired for the night.'

No luck there either - I was beginning to get a bit worried now.

'Where did you use the wallet last time?' asked Jan.

'Well. We had a coffee at the marina, paid two euros for the coffee, but I did not use the wallet for that payment. I had odd change in the pocket to pay for the coffee.'

'Are you sure, absolutely sure?'

'Yes, I am absolutely sure!' Well, now I did not know.

'Before coffee at the marina, we had a meal at the La Fuente and I remembered paying the bill with two €20 notes. The bill was about twenty-five, I left a tip of five, got the balance of change in the pocket. And left. I do not remember about the wallet.'

'You must have left the wallet there. Have you got their telephone number?'

'*No.*'

'Then we have to go there and see if they have it, or you may have dropped it in the car park, outside the restaurant or maybe at the marina.'

Well. It would be one hell of a problem, as all the Spanish and English credit and bank cards are in the wallet as well as Euros, Pounds and Dollar cash, also our driving licences, medical cards, Visa and Mastercard. My whole bloody life's savings! I could see lot of trouble brewing up, trying to cancel all the cards and getting some cash for the rest of the holidays. My heart was beginning to thump full speed, which is no good for my unstable angina.

'Let's go to La Fuente. Down to Caleta.' Jan said.

I don't remember passing the murderous crossing at Almayate, or going through the busy Torre high street either. Just by the blink of an eye we were in Caleta and straight to the restaurant. It was packed and busy with late morning breakfast customers.

'HOLA!'

'BUENAS DIAS!'

'You want something, senor?'

'Have you seen my wallet? It was here last night.'

'Si, *si*, senor! This is your wallet, left it on the table, very nice tip! Mucho gracia!'

'Mucho, *mucho* gracia!' I said, 'Here, have twenty Euros for your honesty.'

'Not necessary, sir. It's our pleasure.'

-32-
Joys and Noise

If you are sensitive and like quiet and tranquillity, do not put Spain as number one on your list of places to visit. It is a country of joys and noise. First of all, the Spanish are an emotional people. They are not calm by nature. They speak with vigour, passion, and make lots of noise whilst doing so. You will think they are always having arguments or slanging matches.

If you see people in a bar having a debate, you may think they're discussing politics or religion – or a subject that ignites passion. But no, often all they are discussing is the price of olive oil.

Day or night, they never run out of things to talk about. They also have canaries chirping all day long. These birds live in cages, which hang out of balcony windows. Their chirrup-chirrup fills the streets all day.

Dogs bark day and night, and sometimes you'll get an orchestra of donkeys, peacocks, and randy tomcats all at it.

On Friday and Saturday mornings, you'll get a carnival of cars hooting up and down the high street, loud music blaring out of their windows. That usually means a wedding, on which occasion it is customary to hoot - letting the world know that the deed is done.

Street hawkers drive by every hour, on the hour. One hoot

for bread at 9am. Two and three hoots for fishmongers calling at about midday. One big blast and two quick short blasts for the grocery man at about 1pm.

Then until 5pm, it's only the dogs and donkeys and bulls. That is a relatively peaceful time - Siesta time. But do not fear, the noise will start again at around 6pm, with motorbikes growling, car radios blaring, and café bar customers bantering about the tango.

I asked one of the village residents, 'Why are you so noisy?'

She said, 'Because we are happy people! Happy people want the whole world to know they are happy. Not like the English who speak through their noses and say *rain, rain and more rain*. What kind of happiness is that?'

-33-
Exhibition Highs and Lows

In September, I returned to Spain and held an art exhibition in Torre del Mar. I think KBL had taken a shine to me because she came every day and helped me open and shut the doors and take in the signboard. It was too heavy for me, due to my angina. The exhibition ran from 6pm until 9pm for 10 days.

It all happened when I went to the council offices to complain about the Green and Stripy store. I met this beautiful lady in the consumer department. Her name was Karen and she was also in charge of art and cultural events. When I told her I was an artist, she offered me this exhibition space at Casa Larios and a champagne reception, to be opened by the mayor. There would be posters all over the town, 500 invitations to all sorts of dignitaries and 100 invitations for my guests, plus publicity in the local press and TV. How could I say no to this opportunity of a lifetime?

Karen also promised a four-page, full-colour artist's portfolio. I was excited and dreaming of fame and prosperity. It took me six months to prepare the pictures for the exhibition. I made 30 canvasses of paintings of the local landscape.

I decided to donate any profits from the exhibition to Seeds for Africa, the charity I was involved with.

I arrived at Almayate a few weeks before the exhibition and went to the Torre del Mar council offices to find out about the promotion and invitation arrangements.

I was told that Karen had left because the grant from the European Community that paid her salary had run out.

No publicity or posters had been arranged. No invitations had been posted to the dignitaries. There would be no opening by the mayor. His name was on the invitation, but they had only printed 100 for me, and the portfolio had been printed on cheap paper.

A council official said: 'This is the key to the exhibition hall and the office and the main gate. You can come at 6pm, open it up yourself, and shut it at 9pm.'

I was stunned and bewildered, with my dreams in tatters. As compensation they offered me as much champagne as I liked. I asked for six bottles. I got three.

I took my 100 invitations and portfolio and played on the fact that the mayor would be opening the exhibition since his name was on the invitation. I invited all the Almayate villagers to the opening day. I knew they weren't that interested, so I had to think of a way to lure them there.

I painted a three-metre long orange tree on a canvas and painted lots of oranges and offered a prize painting if they can guess how many oranges were in the painting. For two euros they filled in a form guessing how many oranges hung on the tree, and the person whose entry got it right would win a painting. All the proceeds of the entry forms would go to the charity.

So as not to rely on the council champagne offer, I also took six bottles of red and six bottles of white of wine. My friend Wayne hung the paintings and we had a fantastic opening. People queued up to enter the orange counting competition. People were counting, re-counting, scratching their heads, asking their wives, partners, girlfriends, boyfriends, children, their mothers and fathers – they were all at it. It was fun.

I also painted some visitors' hands. This is my favourite pastime. I learned it from my stepson's daughter, who is a little darling of two. When she comes to our house in England, she always draws her hand by putting it on the paper and going round it with a coloured pen – what a brilliant idea from a child of two.

I decided to do the same and trace the hands with charcoal, and then with the paintbrush I'd fill in with different colours. You could have blue hands, green hands, yellow hands, and red hands, with black and purple and gold and silver nails. It was a fun thing to do for charity. I still do it now, for parties and on birthdays.

All the women and children waited for their hand painting. We had such fun and were supposed to close the exhibition at 9pm – but we stayed until 11pm.

I managed to sell one painting that day by twisting my friend the estate agent's arm. There was also a couple from England – Jim and Sue. Jim wanted the Balcony of Europe painting, and it was the most popular painting in the exhibition.

When I pressed Jim to buy the painting, he said his boss would have to give him the go-ahead. Okay. I asked Sue for a decision, and she liked another of my paintings, Two Palm Trees. For a moment I thought I'd sell two paintings. But Sue and Jim never agreed which painting they wanted to buy, and so didn't buy either – bad luck for the charity.

After the successful opening – without the mayor – the adrenaline started to flow.

The following morning I made posters by painting palm trees, fishes and flowers. KBL and I went from bar to bar to put up the posters, and KBL telephoned her clients and friends asking them to come to the exhibition.

KBL had an artistic talent. When she was young, she went to Paris and worked for a fashion house where she made a sculpture of shells. A woman called Mathilda, who liked her work, visited her and she got a commission to design some cups with shells.

Later on she found out that Mathilda was Salvador Dali's secretary and agent in Paris. Unfortunately, KBL never managed to have an audience with Dali himself. She did always wonder what happened to the shell cups she designed, and asked me if I could keep an eye out for them, and I've always kept it in mind.

If you see them, let me know, won't you?

The handmade posters were plastered all over Torre del Mar's bars and cafés.

After the exhibition we'd go to a bar or café, get drunk and put up the posters. I also emailed a couple of TV and radio stations. So far one TV Company had visited me, but attendance was still poor at the exhibition.

It was a Thursday, the seventh day of the exhibition, and people dribbled through the door in ones, twos, and threes – only eight people, including two children, had visited.

I started to doodle, do some painting, and KBL turned up with a young Cockney from Dagenham who was doing some building jobs in the area.

He was called Simon. His father is from Iraq and his mother a Jewish lady from London. He got involved in the orange counting competition and gave up after a couple of tries and asked me if I can tell him how many oranges are on the tree. He would not tell anyone, of course. But he was very generous and gave me €10 to go into the charity box and asked me to telephone him on the last day of the exhibition to tell him how many oranges were on the tree.

BOTTLE WATER TREE

-34-
The Old Lady Philanthropist

While we were counting the oranges on the tree, an old lady and her son turned up asking if the local council offices were open.

It was common. Many times I was asked *where is so-and-so's office to pay the council taxes?* and *where are the toilets?*. There was some musical talent competition in the town hall office, and mothers with their children kept asking me directions.

However, this old lady's son, Martin, liked my paintings. They decided to buy Bull On The Hill.

The woman was from Lancashire and they had a holiday flat in Torre del Mar and her husband bought this flat for three thousand pounds in the 1980s. It was now worth 175,000 euros. Her husband had died two years before and left her the property.

Martin wandered off to see the old sugar mills down the road, so we closed the exhibition and headed off to look for him. We found Martin and went to the centre of Torre del Mar to celebrate the sale of the painting. The mother promised to come the following day to pay me. I agreed to pack the painting for her free of charge, so she could take it to England safely.

I had a very nice evening with KBL at the tapas bar. We were at a local bar drinking tinto, and realised that it was 2am. I offered KBL a lift to her marina, which was at least two or three kilometres away. But she insisted that she wanted to walk to her boathouse in Calata. I could not remember where I parked the car. I was not drunk. It was just my age – I forget things all the time. I would spend all day looking for my keys. In the end I'd have to abandon the trip, because I could not find the keys. The bloody keys would be in the trousers I'd worn the previous day.

KBL and I were looking for this car. It took one hour. Eventually I remembered that we left it in the town centre where we dropped Martin and his mother. It makes you wonder how I remember to find my way around my village at 3am. Exhilarated, jubilant and in high spirits that someone liked my paintings enough to buy them, I went home, and made a cup of tea. At last, there had been some recognition for me as a painter. Thanks Martin – you have good taste!

I slept like a log and woke up to the fishmonger shouting, 'The fish are coming.' It had to be almost 11am. It was Sunday. No exhibition today. Had a quick egg and bean breakfast with sweet honeydew melon. I took some medicine tablets, with peach yoghurt, and plenty of tea.

Collecting my writing pad, I headed down to the beach. It was September. All the visitors had gone. Children were back at school. I had the sunshine to myself, the beach to myself. It was more or less deserted, only one or two couples sunbathing.

I was absorbed in writing and listening to the orchestrations of gentle sea waves splashing against the beach stones. This heavy rhythm, it is calming and soothing and lovely like a deep sleep. I had heard the crackle of pebbles and saw a lady walking along the beach, completely naked, top to bottom.

More minutes passed each other by. Later on, I saw a couple rolling on the edge of the water, just interlocking their feet and rolling. They did not have a care in the world: kissing, cuddling and cooling their passion in the sun and sea. How lovely. I could not resist this freedom and longer. I could not continue my writing. *Sod the bloody book*, I thought. I took off my clothes and jumped into the sea and swam, ignoring the couple kissing and cuddling. I was enjoying my naked swim and celebrating the sale of my paintings.

In the end I packed my beach stuff, folded the chair, rolled up the umbrella, beach mat and towel, and got home in five minutes. I had a shower and got ready to go from bar to bar for a tapas celebration.

On Monday at the exhibition hall, I was busy doodling. It must have been about 8pm. Someone tapped my shoulder. It was Martin's mother, come to pay for the painting.

She said, 'Hello Sunshine. I have been thinking over the weekend about your charity, the Seeds For Africa. I don't think I like the idea. This bloody Mugabe. Isn't he killing all our white farmers? I do not want the painting. I have asked Martin and he said he doesn't mind not having that painting with the trees, river and bull on the hill.' Bloody shame.

-35-
Rainbow Anna

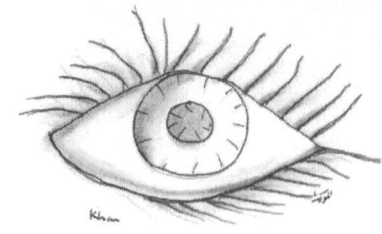

I was sitting in the exhibition hall doodling, bored stiff. It was Friday afternoon, the last day of the exhibition. A lady walked into the hall, looked at the painting, then approached me and said something about the paintings. She said, 'Are you the artist?'

I said to her, 'Are you English?'

She screamed and laughed at the same time, and said, 'Do I know you?'

My brain began to work overtime. I seemed to have some faint idea about her voice. And then she said, 'Aren't you the artist who is suffering from muscle disorder, back pain and unstable angina, who phoned me for help and never kept his appointment?'

I said, 'Yes, I was taken to hospital and was there for nine days in the intensive care unit and could not keep my appointment with you. Sorry.'

She said she had been very worried about me and had sent some prayers and energy for my welfare. 'I am very glad to meet you at last.' she said.

I offered her a seat and a drink from my cool box. Rainbow Anna, as I call her because I know many Annas, had a natural healing practice in Comares. She specialised in iridology. She can look into your eyes and tell what kind of illness you are suffering from. It all started in Hungary in 1837. Ignatz von Peczely found an owl in his country house with a leg injury. He observed that the owl's pupils had white markings, very distinguished and large enough to be noticed by a naked eye. As the leg healed the white markings in the owl's eyes disappeared. At the same time, he was treating a man with a broken leg and he had similar markings in his eyes. The similarity was interesting and he made further investigations.

It works like this: The word iris is Greek and means rainbow. The iris is the colourful portion of the eye that surrounds the pupil. The iris is a complex organ of the eye and composed of hundreds and thousands of nerve endings that are connected by impulses to every tissue of the human body throughout the brain and nervous system. The nerve fibres respond to tissue and organ condition and the slightest change or trouble in any organ of the body is reflected in the iris as lesions and colour variations. A complex iris chart has been developed over many years of research and experience, which guides the practitioner to their diagnostic conclusion on an illness that someone is suffering from, or one which is forthcoming.

Rainbow Anna found meeting me at the exhibition rather overwhelming. Especially when I told her that I had just finished a commission of four paintings for the South Shields District Hospital in the Tyneside NHS Trust. She even got more interested as she was born at this hospital. She believed in fate and stayed with me until the exhibition closed at 9pm.

I decided to treat Rainbow Anna to a meal at the local Indian restaurant. They are very nice people at the restaurant, and come from Azad Kashmir near Rawalpindi in Pakistan. I must say that the food is authentic, tasty and inexpensive. If you come to Torre del Mar and feel like a proper curry, go to Rashid Taj Mahal Restaurant near the old taxi rank.

Rainbow Anna was telling me that the Comares village is very pretty. It was one of the strongholds of the Moorish, and the last to fall. When she came to the village years ago, there was nothing much there and she approached the mayor telling him that she would be setting up a business. He promised her grants and co-operation. She went ahead with all the formalities of form filling with the help of accountants, and opened up a small cottage industry making herbal products: cream, lotion, massage oil blends, and even a café for the visitors. She employed three local ladies but unfortunately, there was still no sign of the grant support.

The EU Grants Office in Brussels informed her accountants that a grant had been authorised and sent through the proper channels to Spain but the mayor insisted that he had not received a penny of it. So the bureaucratic saga went on and on, and Rainbow Anna decided enough was enough. She decided to cut down her operation. She had to let her three employees go. And then she focused only on her naturopathic herbal medicine and iridology.

She promised to look after me and offered to give me once-a-month treatment at special rates – what a generous and kind lady – and a happy ending to the exhibition.

-36-
My Kitchen

My advice to all single people living in Andalucia is *get rid of your kitchen*. I suggest you convert into a spare bedroom, let it out, and dine out on the proceeds.

It will be more pleasurable and less hassle than preparing food and maintaining a kitchen. How much time is spent in the kitchen preparing meals? Just to get a cup of tea you need a clean water connection, a sink to wash hands, a dishwasher to wash cups, a fridge to keep milk, a cupboard to hold sugar and tea, a cooker to boil the water, a waste bin to put your spent teabags in and shelves for your teacups and saucers.

For food you need all this, plus a freezer and a special drawer for vegetables and more cupboards. The list is endless. I bet if you work out the time and cost in installing and maintaining a kitchen, you would find you could eat out like a king.

And that's before you start to think about cleaning the place. What about all the bloody cleaning materials you need? The chopping boards and breadbin?

And all that food shopping! Always I see Anna Senior going up and down to the supermarket. And cooking! I have burnt more toast than the whole of Torre del Mar has had hot dinners. I try to cook pizza under the grill and it is very difficult to know when it is done. Even then, they are never as tasty, soft and creamy as in the restaurant. Mine are stiff, brown and bitter. I have to smother them in tomato ketchup just to be able to eat them.

Have you ever had a stew with fluffy potatoes, soft onions, sweet carrots, spicy celeriac, crunchy celery, mushy mushrooms and mouth-watering chunks of meat?

That's how I dream of homemade stew. But mine always turn out dry and bitter. Not fit for a dog. I only survive it because I drink plenty of tinto with it.

And what did I sacrifice for this kitchen I detest? My car! And not just any car but a super BMW Z3, a darling little sports car, which made people's heads turn on the motorway.

Jan and I used to drive to France and back in that car. And then I sold it. For what? A stupid Spanish kitchen where I would eat burnt toast and dried up stew.

-37-
Drug Drop

One day, I was walking on the beach when I noticed a set of prints in the sand, then another, then some more – until I noticed there were hundreds! At first I thought they were dog paws, as many locals walked their dogs here, but this was like a battlefield. The annual Almayate dog jamboree, perhaps?

Then I remembered. A few days earlier, I'd heard that some criminals had tried to land a boat full of drugs on the beach. The police were everywhere, running through the paddy fields with helicopters overhead. I was on my way back from the garden centre with a car full of geraniums and I had to swerve to miss a police car.

But these marks were too small to be their boots. I was puzzled and continued walking.

Some time later, I turned a curve in the beach and heard a little bell, then another and another. I reached my hand up to my forehead and peered into the sun. Moving ahead of me was a sea of brown goats guarded by one shepherd and a pair of shepherd dogs.

Some of the goat's udders were so full that they could hardly move, their udders almost dragging on the sand. I thought it would be nice if they had a little bra to put their udders in, but I decided against suggesting this to the shepherd and moved on.

Thinking about the drugs made me think back to many years previous, when I had been in Singapore on business. I was at an exhibition when two pretty and confident local businesswomen arrived. They told me they were from a shipping company and I asked them if they could give me a shipping rate for moving goods from the UK to Singapore. I was pleased to have this up-to-date information, so when they invited me to dinner that evening, I accepted. After dinner, they asked me where I was going next. I told them I was going to Bangkok, returning to Singapore, then onto Indonesia, then back to the UK.

They said they had shipping offices in all these places and they would send faxes to their representatives there, asking them to meet me in each city and give me a good quote for shipping costs.

When I arrived in Bangkok, sure enough, I received a telephone call from a representative of the shipping company. We went for a meal at the Bangkok fishing market and had a very pleasant evening. The next morning, I was leaving for the airport, when I was surprised to see the shipping company lady in the hotel lobby.

She said she had called to say goodbye as a matter of courtesy. Then she produced a small parcel, weighing a couple of kilos and asked if I would take it to their office in Singapore, as a favour. I thought it was strange and asked why she was not using DHL. She said it was very urgent and, as I would be there in a few hours, would I mind?

It suddenly clicked and I asked her what was in it. Her face changed and she became quite nervous. Then she excused herself, disappeared and was never seen again!

When I got to Singapore, I tried to contact the shipping company, but the addresses were false and the phone numbers were all out of service.

I had had a narrow escape. Whenever I think of this I get very sweaty.

-38-
Jealous Spanish Lover

There I was one day – on the beach, rolling about on my mat, face all sweaty and body burning, when I heard a thumping sound.

I rolled onto my tummy, still half asleep, and from the corner of my eye saw Saskia galloping towards me on her horse. Saskia was the subject of much village gossip. All the women were talking about her and all the men were dreaming about her. She was Swedish and a juicy beauty if ever I saw one. She was petite with a beautiful round face, blue eyes, and platinum-blonde hair which she always wore up in a bun. She wore denim hotpants and her boobs stuck out like mangoes. She made me wish I were younger. She had been to my art exhibition and admired my paintings, which pleased me no end.

Saskia was married to a local Arabian horse breeder. Apparently she asked for a horse-riding lesson and that was that. She was hooked up with an old Spanish stallion and having the best ride of her life.

A few weeks earlier, I had been in the bodega, wondering which fig to eat next, when I noticed a woman at a table nearby.

'Hello Shaukat,' she called.

'Hello,' I said, not recognising her but not wishing to be rude.

I stole a furtive glance, then realised it was Saskia. She was wearing dark glasses and a scarf that covered her beautiful platinum hair.

I shouted over, 'Why don't you join me?'

'No!' She said.

But I was already up of my seat out of manners. Then she screamed at me: 'Please Shaukat, do not come to my table. I am waiting for my lover and he is a very jealous man!'

Feeling very sheepish, I silently sat down on my chair and quietly got on with eating my juicy figs. It was not long before her lover appeared on a fine Arabian stallion and joined her. She pretended she did not know the old Indian man at the next table. When they got up to leave, and while her lover was untying his stallion, Saskia waved her hand slowly at me and mouthed 'Goodbye'.

I felt very strange. What a grip this old man had on such a young blossom. She once had such a bright future and now she was petrified to speak to her friends. Will it last? I wondered. Jealousy is very destructive. Look what happened to Othello.

So at the beach, when I saw Saskia galloping towards me, I did not know what to do, in case her lover was in hot pursuit on another horse. Saskia got near me, shouted 'Hello Shaukat' and galloped past. I rolled over and went back to sleep.

Hours later, I heard more horses galloping. I sat up in a panic in case they should run me over. Then I saw three tall, young Germans from the nudist club standing completely naked apart from their rucksacks. They were watching Saskia doing tricks on the Arab stallion – her lover was nowhere to be seen.

I felt the cold sea kissing my feet and I ran to the nearest bushes to have a pee.

-39-
Wind-Up

There was an English-speaking radio station in Malaga called Spectrum FM. It had news from the BBC, including traffic reports from London, and played enough of a mix of music to keep everyone happy.

Their best programme was *Wind-Up*, which always had me rolling about on the floor with laughter. The broadcaster, Mike Pearson, would call a local person, an ex-pat, and engage the victim in a hilarious conversation.

One night, I was listening in bed. I laughed so much that I had to get up and stand on the balcony to have a good laugh and get it out of my system. Chippie, my neighbour's dog, thought I was bonkers.

It went like this: 'Hello, Mike Pearson here, golf club secretary. Can you take down your garden fence so our members can come in to collect their balls?'

Homeowner: 'I beg your pardon? Who are you?'

Broadcaster: 'Mike Pearson, golf club secretary. Can you take down your fence so our players can collect their balls? It's very uncomfortable for them to have to climb the fence. Perhaps you could make them an entrance gate? Offer them cups of tea?'

Homeowner: 'I don't believe what I'm hearing! You're saying I should take down my fence or make a gate for your players to come and collect their balls. Do you have a garden of your own?'

Broadcaster: 'Yes.'

Homeowner: 'And would you allow people to stampede through it, then give them a cup of tea?'

Broadcaster: 'What's it got to do with you? You're changing the subject. Are you going to take your fence down? And also, I've been told you have a lot of barbecues, which are quite noisy and disturb our players. Will you be able to ask your guests to keep it down a bit?'

Homeowner: 'Piss off! I don't believe this! What's your name? I'm coming to the club NOW to sort you out.'

Broadcaster: 'Temper, temper! That's not going to get you anywhere is it? It would be very nice if you could co-operate with us.'

Homeowner: 'I'm coming down there to sort this nonsense out!'

Broadcaster: 'Sir, this is Spectrum Radio. You have been on the air for a *Wind-Up*. Hundreds of people have been listening to this conversation!'

Homeowner: 'Really? *(Starts laughing)* Jesus. For Christ's sake. Holy cow. Fuck. Fuck. Fuck!'

-40-
Saint Valentine's Day

In January 2004, when I was due to leave for Almayate, followed by a trip to Pakistan, Jan pointed out to me that not only was I going to be away for her birthday in April, but for Valentine's Day too. She was not impressed, so I invited her to Almayate for Valentine's Day.

Shortly after I arrived at the yellow villa, I was doing a painting of arum lilies on the balcony when I heard on the radio that a five star deluxe hotel was offering special Valentine deals - the hotel Bablos Andaluz in Majis. I rang straight away and made a booking for Valentine's night. Then I emailed Jan to tell her to bring her best outfit and my posh jacket and shirt. She wondered if we were going to a concert.

I picked her up from the airport on February 12 and struggled to keep my little secret. I kept the conversation on her office gossip and the shenanigans of the Almayate residents. She was interested to hear that Anna Bibi had lost 20 kilos and was looking like Twiggy – constantly wearing fashionable clothes and parading up and down the village boulevard like a model.

By the time I was on to the story of next-door's cat being pregnant again we were in Torre del Mar and headed straight for La Cuva – Jan's favourite restaurant. We had grilled swordfish steaks with tinto and finished it off with fresh strawberries. We arrived at the villa at midnight.

Before I left for the airport I put the blow heater on in the hall and hot water bottles in the beds. Jan is a warm person and does not like the cold at all and I had not seen her for three weeks. I took care that nothing would upset her and give her a headache. The following morning we had a fruit breakfast on our sunny balcony, and then Jan admired my garden, which was bursting into bloom.

That day, Jan went to visit friends and I went to my Spanish language lessons. Then in the evening we enjoyed the warmth of an almond wood log fire. I had been collecting the logs all winter. Jan cooked a nice fish dinner for the evening and we drank Spanish red wine.

On February 14th, the big day, we awoke and had lovely English tea, brought by Jan. Then we got ready for our surprise. As we passed Malaga, Jan realised we were not going to a concert. Then we passed the Mijas Country Club and Jan's face fleetingly turned red with panic, thinking we would be playing golf.

Then we arrived at the Bablos Andaluz and Jan looked absolutely delighted. Our suite was a little haven with a spacious sitting room, balcony, bathroom and dressing room, all connected and decorated with wrought iron doors and hanging tapestries.

We spent the next two days sitting on the balcony overlooking the fragrant garden and marble fountain, interrupting ourselves only to visit the spa next door for a sauna and swim before a fabulous Valentine's Day dinner, complete with a pianist playing romantic Spanish songs.

It was so different to the month before – January in England was dull, miserable, dark and cold.

Back then, first thing in the morning, Jan was not in a good mood. She was not interested in small talk as she struggled to get up and go to work. She wasn't happy and I couldn't blame her. I also felt very guilty and uncomfortable that she was going to work and I was not. So to cheer her up, I brought her a cup of tea in bed.

She was listening to the Today programme, with John Humphreys, who was interrogating some clever politician for the nation's delight. No wonder Jan was in a bad mood. I wonder how many marriages have been destroyed by listening to Mr Humphreys in bed?

As I went in with the tea, I smashed my foot into the side of the bed and suppressed a groan.

'You haven't dropped any tea on the carpet, have you?' said Jan.

'No!' I said, as I limped towards her in pain.

'Good!' she said.

I left the room, physically and mentally hurt. There was a time when, if I got hurt, Jan would come running to kiss it better. That was 17 years ago. Before Mr Humphreys changed all that.

I went downstairs, limping and cursing and decided to hobble to the newspaper shop.

I normally read The Guardian, but Jan reads the Daily Mail, so I decided to buy her a copy to please her. I couldn't help noticing a banner across the top of it – Free flights to Europe including Malaga!

That put a smile on my face. I forgot all about my toes, paid for the paper and raced home. Jan had already gone to work, so I phoned her to tell her the good news. I'd worked it out, £9 for the Daily Mail's to get the coupons, then airport taxes - about £20. We were both so happy. She even asked about my foot.

It was a pain to think I'd have to read the Daily Mail for nine days. I'd be like Jan, only wanting straight answers all the time, but it was a small sacrifice to get to the yellow villa for £29.

I had beans on toast then returned to the newsagent to order two copies of the Daily Mail per day, for the next nine days. I was quite excited to be getting something for (almost) free. It would, at least, save me going blind on the Internet searching for cheap flights to Malaga.

Jan and I collected our nine coupons. Frankly it seemed too good to be true. For me, we wanted a return air ticket from Gatwick to Malaga on June 1st, and for Jan one to follow on June 13th. A couple of months later I got a letter from the Daily Mail saying I could call for my ticket. I did, but I could never get through. The line was constantly engaged. I tried for a week and felt increasingly frustrated. I started to realise there was no such thing as a free lunch. For a week, all Jan and I talked about were the free tickets to Malaga and if we were ever going to get our hands on them. Then, one day, I rang and a voice answered.

'Donna speaking, how may I help you?'

I could barely contain my sarcasm and my excitement as I asked her if she was a recorded message. I apologised to Donna for the sarcasm and explained I had been trying to get through for days.

'Yes, we've been busy with the Daily Mail offer,' she said.
I gave Donna the reference number on my letter.

'Thank you, sir. I can offer you a flight to Malaga from Luton at 8am in the morning.'

'I can't get to Luton early in the morning,' I said. 'Can I go from Gatwick?'

Donna told me yes, we confirmed it all and a few days later, a letter arrived. I didn't open it. I just put it away and prepared for the February trip to Almayate and Pakistan.

I came home from Pakistan in May. It was my favourite time of year in England, I wouldn't miss it for the world – blossom everywhere, flower shows and fêtes – I loved it all.

I told anyone that would stand still long enough to listen, that I had got a free ticket to Spain. It was my first good luck of the year.

I realised that the trains didn't run early enough to get me to Gatwick in time for the flight, so I booked into a hotel the night before. It was only £30, so I didn't feel too bad about it. A taxi would have cost £70.

Feeling cool, calm, and collected, I arrived at check-in with plenty of time to spare. I proudly plonked my ticket down on the desk. The clerk smiled.

'I'm sorry Mr Khan. You are at the wrong airport. This ticket is from Luton to Malaga not Gatwick.'

There was no time to get to Luton, so I had to cough up £75 to fly from Gatwick.

Free ticket from the Daily Mail? My arse!

-41-
Wander to Ronda

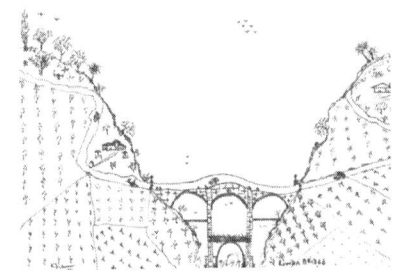

The day after the successful Valentine's night, Jan and I decided to go to Ronda – a very popular destination with all the visitors.

We asked at the hotel reception for directions and they told us to head for the motorway to Marbella and take the road to Ronda from San Pedro.

The journey would take us past Coin, where I had been house hunting and I wanted to show Jan. I'd stayed in a very pleasant guest house near there, run by an English couple from Dorset. They took English money as cash payment and served a Continental breakfast – very hospitable people. Jan and I agreed to go to Ronda via Coin. What a mistake.

The roads were being dug up all over the place, stop-start and all that jazz, and the Valentine's mood had disappeared entirely. It was if I had a strange hitchhiker in the car. The road was turning and twisting, going round a hill and everywhere we looked there were signs telling us we were about to slip down a five hundred metre gorge. Jan was holding onto her seat so firmly that I could see her hands were turning blue.

I did not see Coin anywhere. I had obviously made a mistake. The next sign I saw said 58km to Ronda. My heart collapsed with a little scream. We'd already been on the road for an hour and had 58kms more to go? Good job that by this time Jan was snoozing, or I would have definitely been for the chop.

We arrived in a village and Jan woke up, so we decided to have lunch before heading on to Ronda. Jan asked me how far it was. For the sake of our relationship I said I didn't know, but assured her it couldn't be far.

The landscape around us was very scenic, full of mountains, wild flowers, orange trees and olive groves, but I was concentrating on the twisty and turny mud track of a road, all the time my concentration was attacked by Jan's groans and moans.

We finally arrived at Ronda at 3pm. It took us more than three hours. The view from the natural park was well worth it though and we weren't surprised to learn that the locals had nicknamed Ronda 'The Glorious.'

The city is divided into two parts connected by a bridge. From the bridge you can see the river flowing 120 metres below. If you have not got a head for heights it really makes your knees wobble.

We had a very pleasant stroll, enjoying the Moorish architecture and gardens. Then we found the famous bullring. It is the oldest in Spain and built entirely in stone. There's a museum of bullfighting there. A walk goes from the bullring to the new bridge called Puente Nuevo. It gives you a wonderful sight of the distant rolling hills with olive and orange trees and, on a sunny day, the most breathtaking views imaginable.

The Joy of Roaming in Andalucia

Jan came over to Almayate for her summer vacation.

It was Sunday and I went to Eroski, our local giant supermarket, to shop for a few days' food and also the car needed attention, as the air conditioning was not working at all. It was most important that you had air-conditioned transport in Spain, otherwise travelling is hell.

I also wanted to book hotel accommodation in Cordoba and Seville and organise car hire, as our little car in Almayate was not in the mood for long distance travel.

Last time I booked at the Eroski travel department, it was into the four-star Millie Hotel in Granada and that was a great bargain. So I left the car at the garage to have its air conditioning fixed, then went to the travel agent.

After a long wait, my turn finally came and I noticed that the travel assistant was not in the mood to do business. It was getting near lunchtime and she was in no frame of mind to search for bargains in Cordoba or Seville. She did a few clickings on the computer and that was that.

'They are all fully booked,' she said.

Funny, I thought. Cordoba in summer was so melting hot that even the dogs migrated elsewhere. And now she was telling me all the hotels were booked up. Either she was going bonkers or having an off day.

I smiled, tried to humour her, but it did not work. I left disgruntled and did my shopping in a foul mood. It was a good job I did not come across my friends in the supermarket otherwise it would have been the end of the friendship. I collected the car. Thank goodness they fixed it, because otherwise I think I would have dumped the groceries in the bin and walked to Almayate, and probably died from sunstroke on the melting tarmac.

There was still time, so I went to another travel agent in Torre del Mar. I asked about two nights in Cordoba and two in Seville in a four star hotel with a swimming pool. We needed to be in the centre of town with parking facilities and breakfast. It was no problem. I booked at 80 euros with breakfast and parking – what a relief. I went to the car hire firm, booked a Ford Focus diesel for a week for €221 (unlimited mileage plus insurance for two people to drive) and went home in a happy mood, still puzzled with the Eroski travel assistant's behaviour.

Perhaps her boyfriend had gone to pastures new, because last time she was very kind to me and spent a great deal of time chatting and clicking until she found the bargain. This time, I did not even get a smile. Maybe it was the heat? Though, I do confess, it is a very hard job, clicking away for hours on end, only for customers to walk away and say they will consider it. It is a thankless job. I do not know how they keep their patience sometimes.

Perhaps the customer before me had been on the computer for nearly an hour and said they would think about it. It must have been the last customer that upset her because she is a nice girl. I know she is, because she has a nice face and you can tell a lot about people just observing their faces. I do that all the time. Sitting in cafés watching people going by, looking at their faces and guessing at their lives.

Later that morning I went to Malaga airport to collect Jan. We kissed and hugged and it felt great. It's always nice to see your partner after a few weeks. It's fresh. This is my good advice – if your relationship is in trouble, send your partner away for a few weeks. Do your own thing and give each other a little break. It's nice to be apart and get started again with the same smells, the sniffing, coughing, itching and so on and 'Did you hear what I am saying? You are not listening to me, are you?' 'Yes, dear, I am listening to you.' 'What did I say?' 'Well, say that again. I was concentrating getting out of the Airport.' 'The trouble with you is that you don't listen to me.' 'I do. I do!'

Jan complimented my garden – blooms everywhere. We spent all afternoon listening to each other and talking about English politics.

The following day we spent all our time on the beach and on Tuesday we collected the hire car and went to Cordoba. I let Jan drive the car, it's much easier. I can listen to her while watching the scenery. She is much happier that way, too. She thinks she is a much better driver. I like to let her think that. It's part of the politics of harmonious living, letting your partner think they are great.

We arrived in Cordoba after three hours of driving, just in time for a nice tapas lunch - some potato sandwiches with olives and a glass of red wine. You may say 'yuck!' but honestly, it was delicious. Then we walked around the old quarter of Cordoba and came back late afternoon to the hotel swimming pool and a snooze on the terrace.

At 8pm it was still bright enough for Jan to wear sunglasses. We went to find a restaurant, as ever in search of Jan's perfect formula: it must be crowded with locals and must not do fried food. It must have fresh vegetable dishes, not be expensive, but taste damn good, perhaps with a Michelin star or two. Well it's like finding a needle in a haystack. And as I am a diabetic with cardiac disease, it's difficult to find the right restaurant for both of us.

We were very lucky this time. We found a Spanish restaurant in the old quarter serving excellent house specialities – tuna fish salad and chicken kebab, marinated red pepper and aubergines with honey – to die for with local wine with fresh home-made warm bread rolls. The best part was the bill at a grand total of €24. Don't ask me the name, I can't remember. It is somewhere near the Museo Julio Romeo de Torres. Ask the man in the gift shop outside the museum, Recuerdos el Porto. He is a nice young guy who speaks English. Ask him for a nice place to eat. The area is in the old quarter and is near Plaza del Porto.

After a comfortable evening meal, we strolled along and admired the Cordoba hanging baskets on their Moorish balconies. Spanish guitar music and singing was floating through the air. We followed the direction of the music and saw an old courtyard with lots of people drinking and singing. There were six guitarists and two old local singers. It was delightful. We thought they'd been hired by the wine bar, but when the bar lady complained of loud music, we realised they were just a group of local amateur musicians playing music and singing for their own pleasure. People gathered in the narrow streets and blocked all directions. We managed to find a table with dozens of spent wine glasses waiting to be cleared, so we grabbed it, cleared the spent glasses and made ourselves comfortable listening to the Spanish guitar repertoire and old traditional songs.

It was a very memorable evening and we stayed there until 2am, when finally the musicians all packed up and headed for home. We caught a taxi to the hotel, still drunk with the pleasure of the music.

The following day, we had an excellent breakfast, which Jan still talks about, as they had a special corner for diet freaks and health warriors.

Then we went to the Moorish Mezquita Cathedral – a Moorish mosque and a wonder of the world which holds 40,000 worshippers in its forecourt. Nowadays it is used as a church. We also saw peaceful Alcazar, the Moorish garden. More swimming and napping followed and the next day we headed for Seville.

Twelve years ago, we had a winter break in Portugal. There was such diabolically bad weather that even the locals were fed up. Unfortunately, the hotel was not very good either. Rain, hail, and thunderstorms were the excitements of the day. At night we fought for the hot water bottle and when the thunderstorms came in the night, all the car alarms went crazy. In the end we had had enough and hired a car and headed for Seville.

This time we arrived on New Year's Day and it was sunny. We booked into a four star hotel and had a great weekend. When Jan asked me which hotel we were booked into, I said Fernandez III. She said it was the same hotel we went to twelve years ago. It was quite a coincidence. Sure enough, it was the same hotel, right in the centre of the city - just five minutes walk from the cathedral we had visited twelve years ago. Due to the New Year, everything had been closed, so this time we looked at the Cathedral. It takes a good hour and a half walk around it properly. We met some Americans who planned to see it all in 15 minutes. They did the whole city in the morning and left in the afternoon to some other European city. They did the whole of Europe in a week. That's what I call the cultural tour of a lifetime.

Jan and I did the Red Bus Tour, which was a waste of money. Half the headset sockets did not work, so we spent most of the time hopping from seat to seat, trying to listen. By the time we found a socket in working order, the tour was over. We ended up in the best part of Alcazar Gardens – a haven in the middle of the city. I painted, while Jan went sightseeing.

We'd booked to see Flamenco dancing at 9pm that evening. We found a pizza restaurant near the cathedral; a converted old Roman bath with a Moorish interior, just delightful. The service was fast and the place was full, so we were very lucky to get a table.

We ate a very satisfying, crispy tasting pizza and tagliatelle, with mushroom sauce, washed down with red wine. It was just heaven. Then we walked down to Casa de la Memoria, Calle XI Menez de Enciso 28 and saw Flamenco dancing by Sonia Poveia. Excellent! A highly recommended way to spend one hour, and a Spanish cultural event at its best. The hall was full and you have to book a day before to see the performance. They have different events on different nights and it's always well worth a visit.

Seville and Barcelona city centres are the rip-off districts of Spain for tapas. I am sure these places are designed to catch tourists. They serve tapas in fancy dishes with funny names such as Dali's moustache, Picasso's willy, Gaudi's crusty bread rolls, crocodile salami, blue mountain olives, golden pigs liver, bull's testicles, Malaga giant prawns and so on and so forth. You can imagine people saying, 'Oh, I haven't tasted bull's testicles, let's have some?'

Then it will be served on a fancy dish - two little black balls covered with red shining treacle syrup accompanied with Gaudi's crusty bread rolls and costing €6. In fact it will be two cheap meatballs served from a tin served with a little bread roll covered with sesame seeds.

Be aware the local Spaniards will never go to these places, which usually all have the sign of a Spanish bull hanging from the ceiling and boast that the owner of the bar is a famous matador.

In my village, tapas and a cup of coffee costs one euro and thirty cents and if you have a giant potato sandwich it will be just one euro eighty cents. Tapas is divine, but do avoid the tourist tapas bars. Especially if you have gone to Spain on an economy flight and have yet to recover from the cost of the miserable chicken sandwich and a cup of coffee.

Perhaps it would be a good business idea to offer free flights, then once you're on the plane, lock the door and at

Nerja Caves and Paintings | Nerja Beach

Horse and Carriage, Ner

38,000 feet, auction the chicken sandwich to the highest bidder.

There is a thought for *Jet Express Pizza*. They could have jet scooters delivering pizzas at 38,000 feet. Just call on your mobile and a jet scooter girl will zoom off to your aeroplane and knock on your captain's door with the pizza delivery for passenger number 32 in economy class.

We returned from Seville to Almayate on Saturday. We'd recovered from the cost and taste of the bull's testicles and went to La Cueva in Terre del Mar where we had swordfish, potato, red pepper, grilled red mullet, honey aubergines and wine. We ordered two glasses of Rosé, but the waiter left a full bottle and told us to take as much as we wanted. The bill came to €24 for the two of us and we felt much better.

We had a walk on the promenade, drank some coffee in the various bars and relived our memories of the Cordoba singing choir in the local bar courtyard, Seville's heavenly garden, and the rip-off Red Bus Tour and testicle tapas.

We went home and to sleep and we were woken in the morning by the church bells.

During breakfast, I suggested to Jan that I would like to go to the Competa villa, which is right up in the hills. I had not been there and as we had hired a car, and it did not have to go back until Monday morning, I thought it was a good opportunity to explore.

I also wanted to investigate the Mosaic picture trail. It is the story of the Moorish lifestyle and the ending of their rule in Axarquia, told in mosaic tiles. So that was agreed.

I completely forgot the episode of the Ronda hills trip. The first village was Algarrobo and we just bypassed that village and went on to Sayalonga.

It was a twisting and turning road, Jan was driving and I noticed she was a little nervous. I kept saying how good her driving was. We stopped at Sayalonga and had coffee and a sandwich at the bar. We also had a quick walk around the village, with its incredibly narrow streets. We found two plaques of the Moorish mosaic picture trail and noted down their story, then we began heading for Competa.

It was only supposed to be 16 kilometres from Torre. The road went up and up, twisting and turning and I could see Jan's face was sweating and that she was getting edgy. I stopped saying, 'Wow, look at that view to die for.'

I also have this habit of announcing the names of wild plants growing on the roadside. The area was famous for the varieties of medicinal plants and wild flowers growing everywhere on the hills and on the roadside. The Moors used to export these medicinal plants all over the Islamic world from here.

After one hour of nerve-racking driving we arrived in Competa. There was not a single soul to be seen in the village. We parked the car at the bottom of the village. There were masses of houses piled up on top of each other like a soft ice cream on Irish coffee. But strangely, no dogs, no cats, no one was to be seen at all. We thought it was Sunday, and maybe the cats, dogs and villagers were enjoying their Sunday service. So, step-by-step, we headed up into the village, taking a breather from time to time and catching glimpses of the mountain and sea.

Suddenly, an incredible smell of fresh cooking appeared and we began to follow it. Then we heard humming, like a beehive on the loose. It got louder and louder and the food smell got stronger and stronger. Then we heard some music and as we turned the corner of the street, we saw a mass of people in nice new clothes and children dressed in white holding bunches of flowers.

This was the village square at the top of the hill, with a church. The ceremony of First Communion was in full swing. There were queues to the church, parents accompanying their children and rose petal confetti everywhere.

The square also had four restaurants, with people sitting and watching and celebrating. We were very lucky to find a table at one of them. The table had no shade, so it was very uncomfortable and I was fidgeting and moving from seat to seat around the table trying to keep cool.

The next-door table had wonderful shade, but a single lady occupied the table for four. As I was doing this musical chair thing, Jan shouted, 'For Christ's sake, settle down and enjoy the atmosphere!' The lady's ears pricked up.

'Are you English?' she asked. 'Would you like to share my shade? I am from Birmingham and my name is Priscilla. How do you do? There are five of us here in Competa; we rented a villa, two couples and myself.

'We've had a funny time. I have known Frank for twenty-odd years and we are good friends, me, Frank, and his girlfriend Wendy.

'Then a few weeks ago we met another couple, Jack and Susan and we all decided to go for a weekend in Spain. Frank saw this villa advertised on the Internet so we booked our flight and here we are. The taxi ride up here to this mountain from the airport was quite an experience!

'The villa was quite nice, fully furnished all mod cons with swimming pool.

'The first night, Frank and the other fellow Jack and his partner Susan had quite a few brandies. The party got a bit merry and Frank was getting a bit friendly and frisky with Susan and Jack did not seem to mind at all.

'It made Frank's girlfriend Wendy a bit upset. We thought it strange because I have known Frank all that time and his behaviour with Jack's girlfriend Susan seemed more than friendly.

'But while these shenanigans were going on, Jack tried to get friendly with Frank's girlfriend Wendy. It was getting a bit dark and then we could not find Frank and Susan – they just disappeared.

'It turned out that Frank had a roly-poly with Susan and then it clicked, Frank and Jack had planned this whole weekend just for one purpose only.

'Wendy didn't want any part of it and told Jack where to go, packed up her suitcase and moved out of the villa. It was pitch black outside, but, with her suitcase, Wendy struggled down the mountain to Competa village. Luckily someone was passing on their motorbike and gave her a lift to the centre.

'I'm sure Wendy was quite a sight, with her suitcase between herself and the bike rider and her sitting on the edge of the bike seat praying for her life on every bend. Wendy booked into the local hotel that night.

I am waiting for Frank now. He'll be here any minute. He's gone to the hotel to try and sort things out with Wendy. Then we're all off to the airport. The taxi will be here very shortly. At that moment, Frank arrived and was introduced to us by Priscilla.

He ordered a Brandy and I said to him, 'You'll enjoy the Brandy here. I've noticed it's just two euros, and comes in a bucket!'

'Yes, I need it,' said Frank.

'Why? What's happened?' I couldn't resist saying.

'I went to the hotel where my girlfriend, Wendy, was staying last night, because we'd had a bit of a misunderstanding. But the staff would not give me Wendy's room number. So I left a message for Wendy, asking her to meet me in the bar in the morning, but when I got there, she had already checked out of the hotel and had gone to the airport.

'Apparently she caught the morning flight back home, so we are now just waiting for the taxi to pick us up, the other two, and our luggage from the villa.'

I had to go to the loo then, and when I returned there was neither Priscilla nor Frank. Jan said their taxi had come and they had left.

We ordered our lunch and Jan had a Spanish mixed salad with avocado and I had a local speciality, chicken cooked in local wine with raisins accompanied by potato. It was delicious and a change from fish, fish and more fish.

After lunch we headed for our next village, the Archez and the destination was Canilos de Accituno and then downhill to Velez Malaga and Almayate. As we started from Competa after a good lunch and the amusing Frank and Wendy affair, Jan was in a good mood and offered to drive.

As we headed towards Archez, we came across a wonderful magical Disney-style home. It was real fairytale stuff. We stopped with difficulty, as the road was quite a drop, perhaps a one-in-four gradient. We wedged the car against the wall, in gear and with the handbrake on for good measure, and shoved stones under the wheels.

I took photographs from every angle. I wanted to know who lived there and who had built it, but there was no one to ask. After a time we got back in the car and set off, slowly heading down the car in first gear.

We came to a junction. There were no signs, so we turned right. It was a very narrow road and suddenly the road dropped, making Jan very nervous and she burst out in anger.

I kept calm as I could see we could end up rolling into someone's house.

It was such a drop that you could only see the bonnet of the car. We could do nothing but hope there was still road underneath us.

Slowly, slowly, letting the brake go, inch by inch, we edged down the road for about 50 yards, then came to a flat spot.

Jan put the car in neutral, put the hand brake on and got out.

That was the end of her driving.

'I am not going anywhere,' she said. 'I will walk home if I have to. You and your bloody scenic trip, I've had enough.'

I hobbled out of the passenger seat with my stick, sat in the driving seat, calmed Jan down, promised and crossed my heart not to do another scenic trip, and pleaded with her to go on.

'It's only a few more miles,' I said. 'It's a flat road now, all the way to Velez Malaga.'

I instantly abandoned my plans to go to Canillas de Acetuno.

Thank God – she agreed. I do not know what I would have done if she had insisted that she walked to Almayate. I was pleased and she agreed to sit in the car as I drove to Velez and back to Almayate.

When we arrived back at the villa there was a meaningful discussion about all future hill travel.

I decided to do my book research and take pictures of village scenes after Jan returned to England – on my own!

-43-
Flock of Sheep

Early one morning, I was on my balcony when I heard whistling and dogs barking.

I made some enquiries in the village and was told that the local shepherd was taking his goats to the hills. I decided I wanted to take some photos of this rare practice, so I ran back to my villa, collected my camera and jumped in the car.

I spotted black goat droppings and followed them up a steep track.

Then I saw a little dust blowing, a few miles up the hill. It was a sign. I crept up the hill in first gear. The hill got steeper and steeper and I didn't dare change into second gear in case I lost momentum. The Punto was nearly 12 years old and I couldn't take any risks – at least, not any *more* risks. I was determined to find the goats, so I kept going and all of a sudden I appeared to be at the top of a hill, overlooking a meadow. Within a second I realised the meadow was sloping downwards and I was slipping. I tried to stop the car, but it started to skid. I was terrified and sweating like a pig. I heard myself shouting, 'Shit, shit! Oh God!' My legs seemed to have no strength in them as I pushed down hard on the brakes.

'Any moment,' I thought, 'I'll be crashing down a hundred feet. My body will never be found – what a way to go!'

My mouth was so dry that I couldn't even scream. My hands were wet on the wheel, and then there was a loud bang and a bump. Thank God I had a seatbelt on or I would have been crushed by the steering wheel. The Punto stopped bouncing about. I had hit a *big* rock.

It was my lucky day. I put the handbrake on, put the car in reverse gear and slowly, slowly opened the door and nervously got out. I gathered some stones and put them under the front wheels. Then I got back into the car and reversed it up the hill.

It seemed to take a lifetime, but eventually I was back on flat land. I had some water in the car so I took a drink and washed my face.

I could hear the bells. I turned slowly to my right and there, making a slitting action across his throat, was the shepherd with his goats. His dog came towards me, followed by the goats that started nibbling my shirt.

I began taking some photos. It wasn't my time to die.

-44-
It Drives You Mad

It is easier to buy a castle in England than it is to buy a car in Spain.

What a bureaucratic nightmare. You need patience, you need to be cool, and you need to be passive.

Once you own a house and a car, you are bombarded with official letters from the bureaucrats. Every week, the postman will hand you bundles of letters from officials demanding this and that. I usually ignore them until something drastic happens. It did last week.

A letter from the traffic department informed me that my old Fiat Punto needed its annual road-worthiness test. In Britain it's called the MOT. It can be a death warrant for older cars. It is a good way to keep junk and dangerous vehicles off the road.

In the 1960s there used to be mile after mile of old cars broken down on the side of the roads, with a poor AA man on his motorbike going round the clock trying to repair them, to salvage them from the junkyard.

Thank goodness for the MOT in the UK and compulsory road-worthiness tests in Spain.

I had a month to get my car booked at my local testing station at Algarrobo. It costs about €30 for the test. You make the appointment and then go there on the day with all your documents. You hand in your appointment papers with the correct fee and wait your turn, then off you go with your car into a garage and have your car tested.

You just sit in your car and the tester says, 'Start the engine,' or 'Apply the break,' or 'Put on the right indicator,' and 'Lights on and off.'

It takes about half-hour. And the tester gives you a little sticker at the end, which you paste to your windscreen. The sticker says your car's safe to drive on the road for a year. I don't know what happens if the car fails.

My Punto was 12 years old, and I'd had it for three years. I paid €3800 for it and it has done me proud.

But the old car is reaching the end of her road. The poor girl struggles when going uphill, and really should have been off to the knacker's yard. I decided to buy another car. It should have been straightforward affair. You decide what you want, and go for it. Simple in any language and in any country. Visit three or four car showrooms, see a few cars, ask a few questions, and check the price and what can be offered in part exchange.

And there you have it. No matter if it is new or second-hand, that's what I did in England.

It turns out it is not as simple as that in Spain.

I was looking at similar types of car to the Fiat Punto but with a little more power. The Punto's 1.3cc engine did not pull well on a hill or when I was overtaking. So I was thinking: VW Polo, Clio, Opal, small Audi, maybe a more powerful Punto, or perhaps a Ford Focus.

I went to the dealer that sold me the Punto. I'd been satisfied with the service I received there, and car had given me immense pleasure, and no trouble – not bad for an 11-year-old car. I almost felt guilty replacing her. I felt like an ungrateful lover with a heart of stone, but I did not want to get too emotional. I was only thinking about cars after all. The dealer greeted me enthusiastically with strong handshake, like a long lost brother. I said I'd been pleased with the Punto but would like to buy another small diesel car with a little more power.

'What do you have to offer?' I asked.

He showed me a small Audi, good condition, a 1.9cc diesel engine. He said he could offer me a good deal and also to hand over a decent price for my old Punto in part exchange. He said €2500, even though he had not seen or examined my car.

I asked how much the Audi would cost and he said that as a special favour for an old customer he'd charge €13,500, €2,500 part exchange for the Punto, so the balance would be €11,000.

'And you can drive away your beautiful Audi today,' he said. 'And this offer only applies today as I am clearing my yard for new stock. Even one hundred Euros as a deposit will seal the deal.'

I asked how old the Audi was and he said it was five, maybe six years old.

'It does not matter,' he said, 'as it is a diesel and an Audi - a German make. They hold their value and go on forever.'

He was going on about German cars and their quality and durability. My eye caught sight of a nice, new, silver VW Beetle. It was four or five years old, with 40,000km on the clock. I asked how much and the answer, again, was €13,500. I asked about other cars, and the prices were all similar – all from 13- to 14,000 Euros.

I got little suspicious because the value of old Punto, in part exchange, was in my opinion too high. The €2,500 were much more than other car dealers were willing to offer.

I later discovered, to my horror, that the government offered a scrap value of €400 on any car older than ten years old. Another car salesman at another salesroom had already offered me that price.

I quickly realised that my friendly salesman was upping the prices of his cars by €2,500!

I tried to haggle, offering €10,000 for the Audi, but he would not budge from €13,500, so I called it a day. The next day I sent a friend to the same car dealer. I told her to ask how much the Audi and the silver VW cost. She was told the Audi would be €10,000 if she paid a deposit that day. It was a better deal than I was offered, even with part-exchange for the Punto.

I went to other, more reputable dealerships. But I had no luck getting a better price for my Punto. A maximum scrap value of €750, that's all, and the normal book price for any new car. Some dealers even did not bother to get up from their comfy chairs to show me their cars.

After a week-long search, I found a company demo car - a Toyota Yaris - with a 1.4cc diesel engine and only 400km on the clock – just the job for me. The book price was €14,980, but they were offering it at €12,000 on the road, no document charges, and a scrap value of €400 for my Punto, which was in the end upped to €750. The total deal was €11,250. I tried to get an extra discount of €250, but with no luck. I walked away that day only to go back the next day and ask for the test-drive. I was told to come back in two days time; they were too busy to take me for a test drive. Then I saw another customer arrive and he also showed an interest in the Yaris. I could not face another failure in my search for a car, it was getting too much. I demanded a quick, short drive. The salesman agreed and had a five-minute drive around the block. I was pleased with the performance of the car and paid €400 as a deposit – and that was the start of my Spanish bureaucratic nightmare.

I was told I would have to pay them the full balance payment of €11,250, less the deposit, before they even started to prepare the documents. And it would take about a week or ten days until the papers were finalised and I could drive my Yaris away.

The system works like this: Once you decided to agree to purchase the car of your choice, you pay a deposit. Then they want the balance of payment in full in a few days or on an agreed date. After receiving full payment, they will prepare the documents and submit them to the traffic authority. A week later, if everything is satisfactory, you will have your car – unless your old car has some traffic fines on it that you have forgotten to pay, of course.

Make sure the car you are giving in part exchange does not have any balance of payments outstanding. It will show up on your property documents. All these outstanding fines, and any money due on the old car, have to be settled before the documents for the new car can be processed.

To prepare a car document, the dealer requires your passport to take a photocopy and original papers of the so-called NIE number, which you obtain from your local police station by filling out a form, your two passport-size photographs, and of course your driving licence.

It takes a week to get your NIE number. Without that document, you cannot buy a Spanish car if you are a short or long-term resident in Spain. Lastly, they require a photocopy of your house deeds.

Things got worse when I decided to take out a bank loan to pay for the car. I went to the bank, and asked for a loan. They offered me finance for three to five years. You then need your passport, and, of course, the deeds to your house. The bank charged a 2% one-off fee for arranging the loan and 7% interest over the period you wish to have the loan. In my case I took the loan over five years and I thought it would be straightforward process.

I asked for an €11,000 loan and was told it would be fine and to go ahead to purchase the car. The bank would debit my account with €11,000 and I could pay the car sales room by cheque.

Sun Dried Raisins

Knife Sharpening

The Village Post Office Bike

This sounded simple enough. I went ahead and paid the dealer, writing the cheque out. I was suddenly uneasy about it. So before I signed the cheque, I telephoned the bank worker who had agreed my loan.

However, I was told to come to the bank and see the loan officer again – before I gave any cheque to anyone. I went to the bank straightaway, as it was only half an hour to closing time.

But I was told to come back with my passport and house deeds in two days time even though they'd already had copies a few days before when they agreed the loan. They said the loan document would be prepared and a visit to the notary would be organised to sign the loan agreement, and a charge would be put on my deeds.

Two days later I arrived at the bank at 10am sharp. The documents were ready for me to sign and take them to the notary's office about hundred yards down the road to get it testified by him. The bank made no effort to explain what was in the documents. I signed my part of it, hoping that they were all straightforward documents guaranteeing me my car loan.

When I arrived at the notary office, they asked if I spoke Spanish. I said that I didn't, and they arranged for an English interpreter.

The notary explained that this bank loan agreement for €11,000 for the period of five years was at the interest of 6.5% per year, changeable every year.

I was dumbfounded. I felt like all my teeth had been

pulled out and I had been hanged and drawn and quartered for just trying to buy a car in Spain. I nearly decided to call the whole thing off and tell the bank to stuff their money, but that wasn't either patient or passive. Remember this about Spain: The price is high for sunshine and Hola.

The bank told me that the loan would be at a fixed rate of 7% for five years. Nevertheless, I signed in the presence of notary, and the interpreter countersigned as a witness. The notary's office gave me a paper to say all the documents were signed. I was told to query the interest rate change, but I got nowhere. And I was finally told that I could pay the car dealer.

I returned to the dealership, ready to sign a cheque for €10,850 and drive away in my Yaris. I was expecting straightforward visit. But that was wishful thinking.

'Buenos dais,' said the salesman.

I said hello and then, 'I have come to pay the balance. It that okay? Can I pay by cheque?'

'Yes, you can pay by cheque.'

Ah, a miracle: a straight answer and no problems. Fat chance.

I paid the cheque and got a receipt for it and I asked when the car would be ready to collect.

'Ah, we need your passport and have to keep it for four to five days, and maybe for a week,' said the dealer.

'Why do you need my passport for a week? I am only buying bloody car for God's sake.'

'Because the traffic department wants to see the actual passport.'

'A photocopy will not do? I have never come across such nonsense in my life.'

The dealer, he just shrugged and said, 'Sorry, I have to have your actual passport to get the sales document verified from the traffic department.'

'Okay. I'll give my passport for four days and you have to give me a receipt for it. Can I go home now?'

'No. There is one thing more. Have you paid road tax on the old Punto? I need to have proof of payment.'

I did not have the faintest idea what he was talking about. I didn't know about road tax. Who collects it? Where it is paid? I had no clue.

He telephoned the tax office and was told that the Punto's road tax was up-to-date and paid. This was a great surprise to me. Perhaps when the local council sends you a demand for property tax, the road tax maybe included in that bill. Since that is collected directly from my bank, I assumed that this is how it got paid.

I went home, exhausted, hoping to collect my car on Friday. I was home just an hour when the telephone rang and it was that bloody man from the car dealership. I thought he must like me. Perhaps he was just lonely.

He said, 'Hola, Mr Khan. Do you have road test papers? When is the car due for its test?'

'I already told you when I wanted to purchase the new car that my old Punto is due for test. I'd rather have a new car than renew the old Punto's road test.'

'I need to have notification papers.'

'I do not know what I done with them. I will look for them and ring you back.'

'No, no. I need to have that paper. I will ring back in five minutes.'

He rang back two hours later.

I said, 'Yes, I found that road test notification paper.'

'Mr Khan,' he said, 'you have to go for the road test.'

'It is not necessary as the car is going for scrap. And anyhow, it is your responsibility now so do what you damned well like.'

I slammed the phone down. Well, honestly!

-45-
Magic Dance

One day I decided to go fishing in quite a secluded, lonely spot. Everywhere was quiet and my eyes were fixed on the rod, but I was suddenly aware of movement to my left.

About a hundred yards away, a lonely figure was walking on the rocks. He was jumping from one rock to another, bending down and looking in the spaces in between, scratching each one with a rock he held in his hand.

He was in his 70s, it seemed, and was slim and upright, wearing just swimwear. I realised he was searching for something and the scratching was actually his way of marking each rock.

I was fascinated by his behaviour and reached for my binoculars so I could see him better. I forgot all about the fishing line. He looked to me as if he were performing a religious act or worshipping the sun. Bending down, reaching up, circling slowly, putting his head in his hands then leaping onto the next stone.

As he got closer to me, I could see his face was terribly anxious and from time to time I heard him give a little cry. I must have been watching him for a few hours – this poor soul doing a magical sea dance. Every now and again he became exhausted, sat down, then a few moments later, sprang up and started his ritual of beach-dancing all over again.

I felt bit peckish so I got my sandwiches out, then I walked down to the shore. I noticed something sparkling on a rock. I looked closely - it was a set of keys.

'Some poor sod has lost them,' I thought.

I pondered whether to throw them into the sea, and then I looked back at the old man doing his ritual dance. A little electric sensation ran through my brain and I began jogging towards the man, waving the keys. When he saw me, he began running towards me with all his strength. I could see we were going to collide, so I changed course. He embraced me and tried to kiss me, 'Steady on!' I shouted. He crumbled into the sand weeping, and explained to me in broken English that these were the keys to his caravan and he'd lost them following a swimming session, hours earlier.

He shook my hand and invited me to his caravan for a cold beer to celebrate.

I did not catch any fish that day, but I did find a bunch of keys and a friend for life.

-46-
Antonio the Wise

Apart from the villainous estate agent, there was another Antonio in the village – an elder. He was well respected and the villagers sought his advice in matters of agriculture and property sales.

Antonio made a lot of money as a young man and was well connected. He and I made friends at the bodega. One day, when we were chatting, I discovered that Antonio was diabetic. I didn't see him for a few weeks after that, but someone told me he had a problem with his eyes and was in hospital. A few weeks later, he was out and I saw him drive his Land Rover into a stationary vehicle. People watched, horrified, but Antonio just slowed down, opened the window, shouted 'Sorry, I am Antonio. I have no insurance. Good day.' He drove off. The owner stood there, bewildered, helpless and fuming. Someone told him, 'Forget it, it's Antonio. He's not allowed to drive anymore because his eyesight is so bad. That's why he has no insurance.'

A few weeks later, I met Antonio in the bodega and he told me he could only see me when I was a couple of feet in front of his face. I was astonished and horrified that he continued to drive. What would happen, God forbid, if he hit any pedestrians?

I told Antonio it was dangerous for him to drive and his response was that he only drove very slowly. The thought made me shudder with fear.

I noticed Antonio was limping and I asked him what was wrong. He said he had a small cut on his foot that wasn't healing. I told him to go and see a doctor as his diabetes meant it might get infected and could be very dangerous. I told him it needed urgent treatment.

I got the impression Antonio didn't like going to the doctor's. He assured me he had seen the chemist and all was well.

I went to England then, for a month, and when I returned I did not see Antonio at the bodega. I heard that he was in hospital recovering from having his foot removed.

It was very sad. I really liked Antonio. But I couldn't help feeling it was a blessing in disguise for all the pedestrians of Almayate.

A few weeks later, I met Antonio playing dominoes with his gang of friends in the bodega. He looked happy enough without a foot and greeted me with open arms.

I didn't ask about his driving.

-47-
Nearly Had My Chips

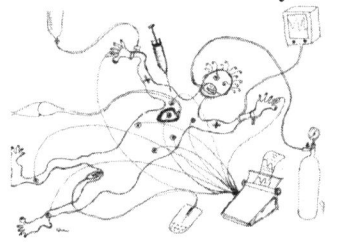

SUR – the free Spanish paper – comes out every Friday with useful news, local gossip, properties and bargains galore from building services to adult relaxation – all sizes available, the choice is yours. Everybody waits for Friday to get this paper.

This particular Friday, I read that Rodney Bewes was appearing at the Nerja cultural centre for one night only. He was a hero of mine in the 'Likely Lads' sitcom in the 70s or 80s. What a great opportunity to see Rodney – and so nearby! So the next day, I dashed to Nerja in my new Yaris (I had finally replaced the Punto, bless her. Thought it best she retired. She must be in some old, Spanish knackered yard or melted down into a metal cube and on her way to China to become a girder for the Olympic stadium. I like to think it's my contribution to world sport.)

I was in Nerja in 15 minutes and parked near the famous Parador Hotel. I walked a few hundred yards to the San Juan Club International, an English den. It has an excellent library, a bar and is a meeting place for English settlers from Nerja and the surroundings hills. It is a cosy place with an atmosphere that's a cross between an old English pub and World War One.

I got chatting to the librarian and told her that my first book, *Breakfast with Figs* was being published and that I'd be happy to do some readings for her members. Her ears pricked up and she asked for a poster. They have hundreds of members. If I sold my book to just one per cent of their membership I could retire (again) comfortably. 'Dream on boy', I thought. 'Dream on.' But life is so beautiful with nice dreams.

I asked the librarian where I could buy a ticket for Rodney's show, and she guided me to Nerja's most celebrated and loved bookshop called W. H. Smiff's. Just come out of the club, turn left, go down to the crossroad, and turn left again at the end of the street, where you will see the post office. Just before post office there is hairdresser called Welli, and there is the Smiff's bookshop. How far is it? It can't be far as I cannot walk for long. Maybe five or seven minutes from the club. But on this day, I could not find Smiff's. I walked for an hour and still no end in sight. I was perspiring like a winning horse after the Derby. I was dog-tired as I walked umpteen times past the post office and hairdressers.

The locals sent me to Timbuktu and back. I was beginning to give up on my dream of meeting Rodney, then it dawned on me – perhaps it is inside the hairdresser's? I was right. I got the ticket, went back to Smiff's where I persuaded them to stock Breakfast With Figs and the owner gave me his email address, which I lost in the pandemonium yet to come.

By now I was so tired that I was feeling some pain in my legs and sweating not just like a horse, but also a pig. So I staggered to the Balcony of Europe promenade, only a few yards away, and sat on a bench. I watched people eating lunch and enjoying ice creams. As they slurped and licked, some of them two cones at once, I began to imagine they knew I was diabetic and could not eat one myself. I could no longer face the hot day and the lack of ice cream so I moved on to my favourite Italian restaurant, a few steps away in the square.

They never disappoint me. I ordered a glass of Rioja and a vegetarian pizza with olives, globe artichokes, eggs, mushrooms and aubergines. There was lots of cheese of course and as I poured chilli marinated virgin olive oil over the perfect, paper thin, biscuit crisp base, I thought how wonderful it was, the way Italians make pizza.

When I finished eating, I was slightly refreshed but still tired. I had a mile walk to the Yaris. Instead of the higgledy-piggledy streets, I took the coastal route and 20 minutes later, knackered again, I took a seat in a little courtyard garden, where I relaxed for a while, reading the newspaper.

I was there only 10 minutes when I heard an almighty row between a Spanish couple in a nearby flat and felt it was time to move on, despite my legs refusing to budge. With the help of my stick, I dragged myself to the car and headed for Almayate, dumped the car in front of the villa, blocking the road, and went inside.

By now, the pain in my legs was making me scream. I wished Jan were there to massage them. I would have gladly massaged her feet in exchange. That was her favourite treat.

My whole body, every muscle, was in turmoil, so I took extra Ibuprofen and went to bed. At 6pm, I woke up, still sweating, and decided to take a shower. I made myself a cheese and tomato sandwich, drank a cup of tea and went

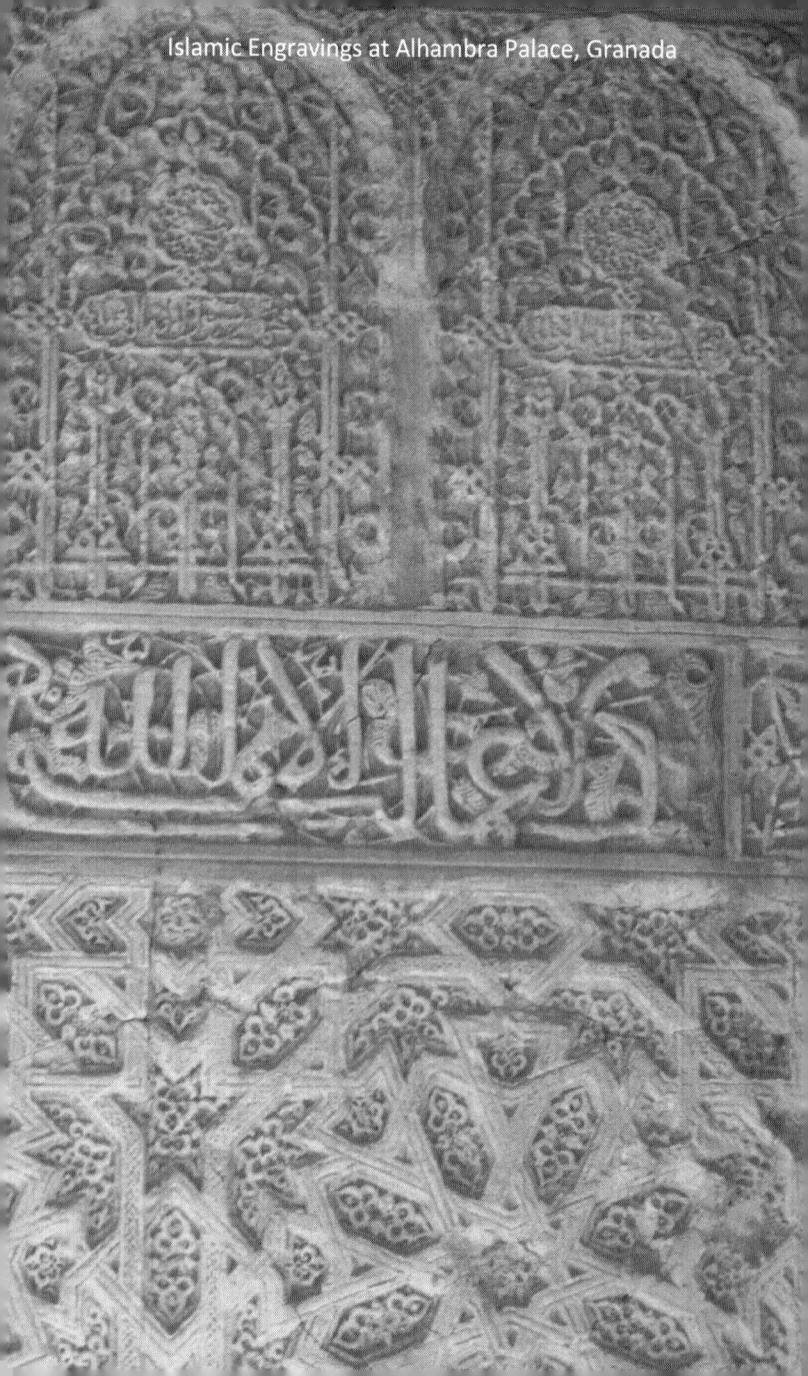

Islamic Engravings at Alhambra Palace, Granada

Islamic Engravings at Alhambra Palace, Granada

to see KBL and Penny at the tapas bar where we had arranged to meet.

I started to feel better when Penny told me how healthy I looked and I ended up staying until 1am. I had one glass of Rosé and one coffee. It was such a great evening, one in a million, as the weather was perfect, rather delicious in fact, warm with a slight cool breeze from the sea.

We looked over the floodlit flowers and palm trees, talking rubbish, clearing our brains to start again the next day. At 1.30am, I went home and went to bed, with a glass of water.

At 4am, I woke up with an almighty pain in my chest. I thought the tapas might have affected my stomach, so I took some Ibuprofen. It always works. But not this time. Starting to feel worried, I sprayed my Glyceryl Trinitrate and tried to keep calm. But it was no good, I couldn't sleep, so I got up and went downstairs to finish writing the final chapters of *Breakfast with Figs*, spraying as often as I was allowed.

Eventually I was tired and went back to bed. At 9am the phone rang, it was Jan.

'How are you darling?' she said. I was not going to let her worry, a thousand of miles away, so we had little chat before she went to work and I went back to bed still uneasy about my chest. I twisted and turned, then went downstairs to eat an enormous onion omelette. I couldn't eat it all, so next door's cat was pleased.

I carried on writing, the final touches – done! Anxious that Sparkle should have it before I pegged it, and against my better judgement, I began the drive to the Internet café in Torre.

My heart now felt as if someone was squeezing it like a chef squeezes a lemon, but with an enormous, burning hot hand. I realised I'd forgotten my spray – how stupid could I be? I emailed the chapter and drove home. Normally it took me 10 minutes to negotiate the underground car park near the villa, but that day, I drove straight into a space, went into the villa and called Wayne, Coral's husband and asked him to take me to hospital immediately.

Five minutes later, as I was standing outside the front of my villa, I saw Coral and her oldest son, Rashid, driving towards me. She got out and started asking me all sorts of questions, but I had started to panic, so I said, 'Just take me to hospital quickly, I cannot talk, I have a serious heart problem.'

In dead silence Rashid opened the back door and helped me into their jeep. Normally at 2pm, the roads are empty like a ghost town, but – sod's law – the traffic was like I'd never seen it before.

All of Spain seemed to have abandoned the Siesta and was out on the roads and every traffic light seemed stuck on red.

We also ran out of petrol on the way. In all, it took us 35 minutes and should have taken no more than 10.

At the emergency department they wanted to see my passport. I said I was having chest pains and would show them later. That did not go down well. She gave me the Spanish look. As I rummaged in my bag, I found my NHS foreign travel card. It was a sight for sore eyes! I was immediately carted off, checked by the doctor and connected to the cardiograph machine.

The graph was crazy, up and down, up and down, with one line sticking up like Mount Everest.

'How do you feel?' said the doctor.

'Bloody marvellous, never better, what do you want me to say?' I snapped.

I was dying for a sip of water, perspiring like a pig and moaning like a baby.

Next thing I knew, I was stripped naked, my clothes given to Coral who was ushered out, and on my way to theatre. I don't know what happened next.

When I woke up two days later, I didn't know where the hell I was.

Faces peered over me.

'You had us worried, Shaaakalt,' they said.

'It's Shau-Cat,' I managed to say.

'Oh, Nameste, are you Indian, Show-Cat?'

'No, I'm Chinese,' I said.

'Lovely to meet you,' said a face I now recognised as the doctor.

'You are a brave man. You have not lost your sense of humour despite your heart attack.'

I missed the bloody Rodney Bewes one-man show but I am lucky to be able to tell this tale.

I did finally see Rodney in my hometown, Canterbury, where he appeared on stage. It was worth the wait.

And I must say the expertise and dedicated care of the Torre hospital was second to none despite our many misunderstandings due to the language barrier. When I asked for the pee bottle, I got a bottle of water, when I asked for water, I got the pee bottle and when I wanted to go for the Big One, I got the pee bottle again.

In the bed next to mine, bless his heart, the patient was letting off wind for Spain. To be fair, I was snoring so much that the poor chap couldn't get a minute's sleep. One night he even told me to put a sock in it.

He was very ill and his wife and daughter were there giving him 24-hour care, full of emotion and tears, as he was not expected to live more than few days as he had advanced pancreatic cancer.

I felt quite guilty for keeping him awake. I tried to put a peg on my nose, but it did not work. I hope he forgave me. When I left, I said I would pray for him. But it did hurt my feelings when one of their English visitors told me I shouldn't have been there, getting care. But that's some people for you – speaking their minds before knowing the facts.

When I got home from the hospital at midday on Friday, I caught a taxi and was home in 10 minutes.

Anna Senior had cleaned the house from top to bottom, made my bed and cooked chicken broth and apple stew. I couldn't have wished for a kinder neighbour.

I also had visit from KBL, who supplied me with bottled water and kept me amused and my spirits up. Coral had also been wonderful when I was in hospital, bringing fruit, clothes, slipper, pyjamas and toiletries.

I rested all day in bed, then that evening went to the coffee bar with Carol to relax and count my blessings.

I met a strange Irish woman called Pauline there. She had heard on the grapevine about my heart attack. 'Shame, you're still here, we'll miss your funeral drink now,' she told me.

Very comforting indeed. This world is made of all sort of interesting people. Long live Spain and all the people in it.

-48-
Adios

I came to Almayate on the 20th day of June in the year 2002. I fell in love with the place instantly and that was that.

It is modern in some places but rather rough and higgeldy-piggeldy in most. There are caves on the Black Bull Hill where some gypsies live quite happily. It is the most amazing village where dwellings, houses, modern villas with swimming pools, cortijos and farm sheds, donkey and horse stables are dotted high and low in the hills with whitewash shining like diamonds among miles of twisted dirt tracks going through groves of mangoes, pomegranates, wild almonds and cultivated avocados. In the centre of the village you will still find people living with their cattle, donkeys, goats and pigs. Lots of streets are still just bare dirt tracks waiting to be done up and yet there are beautifully paved roads alongside ankle breaking, leg twisting unmade pavements, covered with dog shit, horse dung and goat droppings.

You are walking along, on a nicely paved pavement and all of a sudden you come to the bus stop near the entrance of the Lo Popemolinos restaurant and you struggle with your walking stick to stay upright on the unmade pavement. I am sure people think you are drunk with the tinto and struggling to catch a bus. In matter of fact there is no pavement but an unmade scruffy mass of concrete lumps thrown on the path by some drunken labourer. The local council have recently spent thousands of Euros to put up a drinking fountain on this unmade lumps of concrete. It's only useful to the shepherd and his sheep when they pass it early in the morning on their way, going to their new pasture to the hills. Humans can break their legs while trying to catch few drops of water in mid air, and then fall flat on their back on the uneven concrete surface. It's a good place for the village dogs to put a leg up. It has become the meeting place for all the dogs in the village: 'Hold on baby, I just put my leg up on the fountain.' 'How about I show you mine and you show me yours?' It's been four years since I have been back and this is the heart of the village, the entrance to the most popular restaurant of the area, the bus stop, the lottery kiosk, the newly erected drinking water fountain, the village bank, the agricultural supply depot, the coffee bar, the dogs' personal leg-up meeting place, but no pavement. Perhaps the council have a blind eye for this spot and yet they have spent thousands of Euros up the road twenty yards away, making a beautiful surface where the village dustbins are kept. Well, this may be some Spanish politics I'll never understand.

I pay my council taxes as anybody else but I am fed up with unmade pavements and dirt tracks in the centre of the village. My villa is a hundred yards, maybe less, from the supermarket, bakery, bank, fishmonger, chemist and coffee bar. Fifty yards from my villa is very nice concrete road, which Anna keeps it cleans by washing with water from a hosepipe daily (water shortages are so serious that sometimes there is no water for a couple of days). Then it joins to the unmade dirt track, boggy and muddy due to Anna washing her upper side of the road. I have been hearing that the council are going to make the last fifty yards into a good concrete road very soon as seven modern town houses have just gone up whose residents will be soon using this dirt track, but I am sure this bloody muddy, slippery track still be there if I came back in ten years. Strangely, I'm beginning to like this rural charm of slippery muddy roads, pavements covered with dog shit, horse dung and goat droppings, supermarkets with customers smoking cigars, ham sandwiches served and made in the restaurant with unholy unwashed hands and coffee with cockroaches for that little extra crunchy taste.

To give credit to the cleanliness, once in a blue moon you can see a road sweeper with a long hose in his hand spraying like a mad man, or maybe a lorry spraying water onto the pavement to make it more slippery - even the dogs don't walk on the pavement as if they know they may break their leg by slipping on their own golden nuggets. It's not like England where you are walking along behind your doggy with plastic bag and a scoop: 'come on boys, for God's sake do it! Hurry up! I have to go to work! Do it now boy, be good boy so I can scoop it up!'

Once I was on the way to Lo Popemolinos for my breakfast when a giant dog confronted me as soon as I came out of my villa gate. He showed me his teeth, growled and went for my leg. I defended myself with my walking stick and legged it towards the restaurant a couple of hundred yards away. By the time I arrived at the restaurant I was chased by six or seven more of his friends. How I swore! I had been looking forward to a nice coffee but in sheer desperation and fear I ordered a large brandy and the barman was taken back the choice of my morning drink. Can you imagine? In my anxiety I spent the whole afternoon at the restaurant to recover from the dog chase, and not a single Spaniard came to my rescue. He was a big Saint Bernard dog and I think he was the village 'top dog' and gang leader: when he barked his disciples all appeared from nowhere to join him in the manhunt. I often saw him at the drinking fountain with his mates and several female admirers. I also noticed that he did not bother local Spaniards and blond people, he just didn't like black or Moorish folk, so the trick was to go around with a nice blonde. So if you are rather friendly with a blonde and she is happy to accompany you to the restaurant than this is the right place for you to live.

I'd get up six o'clock in the morning, go straight downstairs, make a cup of tea in the kitchen, warm a croissant in the microwave and take them to my study corner in the sitting room. I'd open the courtyard window and sit on the table and start writing my manuscript. You get the fresh smell of jasmine, frangipani and orange blossom, a view of the glorious colours of purples, pink, red, blue and white of bougainvillea and hibiscus. You can hear wild finches chitchat sitting on the electric pole and canary songs from the next-door neighbour's courtyard. It is a magic time to write. Your mind is fresh and alert, not contaminated by dog chases, hawker's cries, donkey's honking, 'he haw, he haw', and pigs screaming. I'd type away on my laptop till nine-thirty when the bakery van comes in and blows my eardrums with his horn. I'd then have a shower, dress and have more tea and take the medicine (now about eleven tablets which keep my heart pumping away). Working for one more hour than it would then be eleven-thirty, time to walk down to Lo Popemolenos.

If unmolested by the Saint Bernard and his mates, I'd order Tostada tortilla (toasted egg sandwich), coffee con leche, olives and tapas of sweet chillies. I would sit on the restaurant patio under the shade of the fig trees. That Mediterranean blue sea in front and to my left ranges of mountain covered with avocado groves and black bull hill with its caves and kestrels hovering to pinpoint the odd snake or mouse, ready to dive and scoop for his breakfast. It is another magic moment, with the cool breeze from the nearby eucalyptus and my iPod playing enchanting larks, the soul is in heaven. I love these moments reflecting past and present and considered myself to be blessed. This is the time I get inspirations for ideas and stories and sometimes I will make small sketches for future paintings. You are watching bulls ploughing the fields, goats are grazing over the mountain, a line of horse riders exploring the mountain scenery and if you're lucky you will see that kestrel dive to pick off a snake who is resisting by wiggling his body and tail hopelessly.

Recently, a small terrier who is not a member of Saint Bernard's clan has started to appear at my breakfast table at the restaurant patio garden. I call him Buddy. Still harnessed and on a broken lead, he begs and shares some of my odd breakfast morsels. He can stand up on his rear feet and look at me with his tongue hanging out, so how can I turn down his request for some food? When I give him some dried up bit of toast, he picks it up with his mouth and goes round the table jumping with joy like a footballer who's just scored a important goal and is running around on the pitch like a headless chicken jumping about in front of his supporters. One day I was late and he was waiting, patiently curled up under the table. As soon as he heard the noise of my walking stick, he started to waggle his bit of a tail and went jumping with joy from table to table. I had to calm him down by putting on the floor a saucer full of coffee. After his coffee and toast he just goes away - disappears into thin air. I made several enquiries in the village to meet his master but failed in my mission.

There are dozens and dozens of dogs in the village, in the houses, in the street, in the fields, in the restaurant, yes, in the restaurant - Spanish ministers must have ensured a place for their dogs in the treaty of Rome that Spanish dogs must have the right to enter the restaurant at all times with dignity, the right to snatch breakfast, lunch and dinner, a right to snooze under the table and a right to bite any customer who they did not like, but they have no right to lay on the beach, catch fish, play games like fetching stick from the sea, fetching ball, joining in with the beach volleyball games, or represent Spain in the Olympics. Dogs are denied all these rights and to police this part of the treaty the council have a dog catcher patrolling the beach who you see once every three or four years exercising his duty catching stray dogs, and playing with the children making sand castles, nicking beach bather's sandwiches, paella and drinking their ice cold beer. I was lying on the cool sand on the edge of the beach, enjoying the sea waves kissing my feet time to time; it's almost a feeling of immense sexual pleasure without actually having sex on the beach. Try it sometime - you do not have to grovel to your girlfriend for the favour! I was in heaven adding to the pleasure by listing to the Penguin Café on my iPod. Then I heard a loud commotion and people running, children screaming, dogs barking but the centre of attraction was a struggle by two men holding Buddy's tail and pulling it a tug of war, all beach dogs one side and two dog catchers on the other side. For spectators all the dogs of Almayate, including Saint Bernard's gang. I was horrified! I tried to stop the dog catchers taking him away because he played with me for three years on the beach; we grew up together and enjoyed our walks, discussed our girlfriends' problems, spied on drugs smugglers on regular basis and swam together in the sea. However, as he was not my official dog, only adopted, I had no right to stop his execution. Children, women, men all had tears in their eyes as nobody claimed him as their dogs. Buddy begged for mercy. He howled and howled: 'I don't want to go, please save me! I want to stay on my beach I am no burden on the taxpayer. I eat all the dead fish on the beach, keep it clean for the bathers!' His protest was in vain, we all saw white dogcatcher van disappear over the horizon. Bloody sad.

Mudejar Tower • Village House in Archez

Competa Village

It's been tough to go to bed at night ever since I read in the local paper that thieves were found in the wardrobe. Well I ask you! Honestly, I am not making it up, it's all true - thieves found in the wardrobe. Really, you do not expect to open your wardrobe after the shower, standing stark naked in front of the mirror, making funny faces, trying to assess your body's good physical points, measuring size of your willy, opening your mouth, checking the sharpness of your teeth, taking out your tongue and kissing your shoulder (have you tried it? You will now.) Investigating spots on your face and squeezing blackheads, taking out that horrible yellow muck, making yourself feel better after a little pain, smelling your armpits. Phew, then sliding the wardrobe mirror door to get your pants when instead out leap two giant horrible looking blokes with machetes in their hands going for your head? Your willy shrinks to the size of a peanut and you are running for your life from room to room! To the balcony, then downstairs out through the front door to the courtyard and out into the street! You're on the run, shouting, screaming, covering your peanut-size willy with your hand as best as possible, then you feel the warmth of your piss running down your leg due to the fear you missed a sharp machete blade by the whisker of a hair.

The story had it that the Torromolinos police have arrested two men. Apparently the residents of the house were fast asleep and woken up by the police officer knocking on their door. They opened the door and the police searched the house in pursuit of two dangerous criminals. They searched the whole place from top to bottom and failed to find these criminals until a bright copper searched the bedroom where the family had been sleeping. To the police officer's surprise they were hiding with machetes in their hands in the wardrobe.

Now I am in constant fear, checking my wardrobe inch by inch before going to bed. I turn in my bed so I am facing towards the wardrobe doors at all times while nodding off to sleep. Sometimes I dream that Dali's tiger is leaping out of the wardrobe and catching me by the throat, blood shooting out from my aorta like a fountain and I am drifting too far, far away to unknown darkness. The slightest little noise makes me jump from the bed. I go to every room in the house, check every window shutter, the space behind every door. I am going up and down the house like a lunatic in the middle of the night. The only good thing to come out of this saga is that I have lost one entire stone. As soon as sunrays penetrate into my window I close my eyes and sometimes do not get up until late in the afternoon. People in the village think I am dead, and come knocking on my door, and my stray dog waits at the Lo Popemolinos for his coffee and tortilla.

Now I am also petrified of collecting any of my visitors from the Malaga airport. I just tell them that I am not feeling well and that they should catch a taxi. I cannot collect them from the airport. Lately, police at the airport got very tough with the unlicensed, self-appointed taxi drivers, who are touting for business and picking up fares, especially from English holidaymakers. Recently an angry looking Spaniard caught up with an English man at the airport who was collecting his visiting friend and got a shock of his life when he told him in no uncertain terms that he was running an illegal taxi service for the English visitors. The Englishman got very upset by this accusation and went to the airport police station to lodge a complaint against this unfounded charge, this fool playing at policemen and to satisfy his honour and the injustice of the accusation without any firm evidence. He was told at the police station that he had been seen on the security camera quite often picking up passengers. He told them that he has many visitors from England, and he likes to pick them up personally and that it is perfectly legal and he does not like to be accused of something he has not done. His pride, honesty and integrity are at stake.

His car documents were checked and he was given a Spanish written statement to sign, which he did and left the airport with his visitor with his honour and pride intact, but it did not last. He was gobsmacked when he received within a few days a letter from the town hall of 1500 Euros fine for being at the airport without permission, I presume for running an unlicensed taxi service. He intends to fight his case, but the moral of the story is not to sign any documents or papers which are written in Spanish if you do not understand the lingo. Ask for the English translation, and it is your legal right to have one provided.

A similar thing happened to an English restaurant and bar owner. She decided to sell her bar and put it in the hands of various estate agents. One day over the early part of the weekend when she was very busy serving the customers, a newly appointed estate agent arrived waving a piece of paper for her to sign as she was very busy told him to go away and come back another time. He insisted that he needed the authorisation to sell as he had many customers waiting to inspect her restaurant with a view to purchase, so she signed without reading the small print in Spanish. Months went by and she sold the restaurant through another estate agent, paid his commission and everything was hunky-dory until she received a demand for the sale commission due to the previous agent. It turned out she signed away sole exclusivity to him on that busy day. She had no choice but to settle his bill of few thousand Euros in the local court. Beware, as they will take your shirt while you're having tapas!

I was having cramps in my legs at night. I had forgotten to bring my tablets for cramps from England. I spoke to Jan on the phone to send me few tablets by first class post, expecting to arrive them in few days. I was not so lucky; days gave way to weeks and weeks to months. Since then I have been to England and back to Almayate. One day a bundle of letters was delivered by an English family living a few hundred yards away. 'This is your post Mr Khan.'

'Why the hell did the postman not put it in my letterbox?'

'Well he always gives me all the post of the English people living in the village when I go to the supermarket for shopping.' The postman just stands there with his 1920 motorbike loaded with supermarket carrier bags with post dangling from the bike handle and he is handing out bundles of post to any person going to the supermarket for shopping. These bundles of letters are not for the individual person but one bundle for each street resident: whoever happens to be coming out for shopping for a 'quicker' distribution.

I opened the post, now several weeks old. I had missed my dinner and gala ceremony at the Malaga town hall in recognition of my thirty-six meter long multicultural mural, which was painted by myself with other eighteen artists for the Malaga town. I also found my cramp tablets three months too late.

Perfect.

I had been away nearly three months to England recovering from my angina operation and could not risk any air flight hassle. On my return to Spain, I was surprised to see a very high level of electricity consumption. I could not get my head around the reason for this huge electric bill. Later, I wanted to do some washing and the washing powder was nowhere to be seen in the laundry room. My electric drill, tools and ladder were also missing. I was discussing this strange disappearance and the shockingly high electric bill with my English friends at the coffee bar and I got a sudden quietness about the subject, nobody wanted to know. Finally somebody cracked up under intense interrogation, and said that the culprit is very close to my heart. As soon as I left for England she all but moved into the house. My balcony is used for drying her washing and if any repair in her house needs to be done, an electric cable snakes through my house to next-door, humming away, powering my tools.

I was fucked good and proper. I had had it with drinking almond milk saturated with garlic and gazpacho soup with strange looking bodies floating on top. I do know she means well, she looked after my plants. She cleaned my house, made my bed, did my laundry and ironed my clothes and she kept an eye on my house to ensure nobody came in and hid in the wardrobe with a machete. Mine was the only villa in the whole Axaquaria which is safe from robbery due to her vigilance and not to forget she saved my life by getting her nice to take me to hospital when I had my angina attack. Bless her. I will be overlooking this electric bill, but it is the principal of it. She only has to ask for it as her family always comes to use my microwave to make popcorn.

All the residents in my hamlet have been asking my English friends who speak fluent Spanish why I want to sell my villa, how much I am selling for, where I am going, who will look after me and my needs, washing cleaning and feeding, so on and so on. To make me feel even guiltier they organised a sardine barbecue in my honour for being such a good neighbour (and also to have the chance to wring out some more information about my departure). One couple even went to the trouble to bring their niece from Malaga to interrogate me. We had a wonderful sardine barbecue with lots of Sagria to drink, olives, tomatoes, and sardines grilled on an open fire. I myself was grilled by the beautiful young senorita but I did not crack up, and decided to have good time instead. I woke up in the morning smelling strongly of sardines. Phew! I had to be careful not to go to the beach otherwise I would have been attacked by the seagulls.

The last two years have been hell, what with the construction of seven town houses in front of my villa, hammering, drilling, squeaking, lorries coming and going, reversing and breaking my flower pots. Concrete mixer crackling eight hours, day after day. The houses are nearly complete and now, in the next street twenty yards away, a couple of old single storey huts have been knocked down and three storey blocks of flats are going up. The tranquillity is lost and I cannot face another two years of hammering, drilling and knocking starting at seven in the morning. I want peace.

I will miss Anna, my patio garden, sea views, the walk to the beach going through the sugar cane and sunflower fields, breakfast with figs at the Lo Popemelonos. I will miss the fragrance of jasmine and eucalyptus, the gorgeous colour of bougainvillea and hibiscus. I will miss listening to the bells of the sheep grazing on the Black Bull Hill, walking to the country through streams and picking up wild almonds, pomegranates and olives. I will miss watching the kestrel hovering in the sky and diving to pick up odd mice and snakes. I will miss watching the deep blue Mediterranean Sea and the fish jumping, chased by dolphins. Farewell, Almayate, you will always have soft and loving spot in my heart. I will dearly miss watching the view of the sea from my balcony, seeing boats sailing out of the Calata harbour in the evening and sailing back in the morning laden with their heavy catch of fish, chased by hundreds of seagulls. I will miss the songs of the canaries.

Farewell, Almayate.

Adios.

About the Author

Shaukat Khan was born in Jullunder, East Punjab, India.

Shaukat came to England, from Lahore, Pakistan, as a champion swimmer. He represented his country in the Butlin's International cross channel swimming race of 1959. He worked briefly at the Wellcome Foundation Research Laboratories in Beckenham, Kent. Then he established his own herb farm in Canterbury, to research and develop herbal products.

The herbal products were exported to 44 countries across the world. Shaukat had hundreds of employees and two factories in England and Germany. Clients included The Body Shop, Harrods, Fortnum and Mason in England and Fauchon in Paris.

In 2000, unexpected cardiac health problems forced Shaukat to retire and develop his first loves of art and writing. He has exhibited at the University of Kent, Canterbury, The Mall Gallery London, Abbeville Tourist Office (France), National College of Arts and Coopera Gallery, Lahore (Pakistan) and in Malaga, Spain.

In 1979, Shaukat published, Herbs: How to Grow and Use them, a bestselling book which proved so popular that it was translated into many European languages. It was published by Thorsons, now part of Harper Collins.

Commissioned works by him can be found at the South Shield's NHS Hospital and Rutherford College, University of Kent, Canterbury – where he has been made an Honorary Senior Member.

The author contributes funds from the sales of his paintings to UNICEF and the charity Seeds For Africa (SfA). He recently travelled to Kenya for SfA to set up their Garden of Goodness project – where small farmers can get seeds, knowledge and practical experience in growing their own organic medicinal plants and vegetables to improve their lifestyle, living standards and help alleviate poverty.

In nearby schools, the Garden of Goodness project teacher helps students grow their own food to alleviate hunger and learn about agriculture.

In Pakistan, Shaukat organised an environmental workshop called The Importance of Trees. Two hundred students from the National College of Art (Lahore) helped him create nine installations in a public park for thousands of visitors and millions of TV viewers.

Art critic Dr Paul Easterbrook, lecturer in History and the Theory of Art says:

'I have become well acquainted with your work. I have much enjoyed the bold colouring especially, which has clear affinities with so much of the painting of the past-from Matisse and the Fauves to the contemporary environmental work of Andy Goldsworthy and you have a great deal to offer in so many contexts.'

Art experts now recognise in his paintings the passion of vibrant colour and the excitement and energy that can thrill and delight the heart.

To see his latest work visit www.khanart.co.uk